"I see someone else likes to take moonlight walks," Justin spoke from out of the shadows.

"Yes . . ." Jennifer answered softly, her momentary fear replaced by a shiver of excitement at his presence. Looking up, she could see his rugged profile silhouetted against the fragile delicacy of the pagoda.

"Come here," he said gently, his voice low with emotion.

Jennifer mounted the narrow steps, taking the hands he extended to her.

"It's beautiful here in the moonlight," he murmured, "and you are beautiful in the moonlight." His mouth descended on hers, his arms wrapping around her softness to pull her close. His lips spoke a passion that devoured her in its fire, robbing her of every feeling except a stunning ecstasy . . . .

Forbidden Memories

Annette York

GOLDEN APPLE PUBLISHERS

FORBIDDEN MEMORIES

A Golden Apple Publication / June 1985

Golden Apple is a trademark of Golden Apple Publishers

All rights reserved.

Copyright © 1984 by Annette York.
Cover photograph by Photofile

ISBN 0-553-19774-6

PRINTED IN THE UNITED STATES OF AMERICA

O   0 9 8 7 6 5 4 3 2 1

Forbidden
Memories

One

The narrow, crowded streets of New York City's Greenwich Village were alive with people on the first warm day of spring. Everywhere the air held the feeling of promise, of a bright, new beginning, yet Jennifer Montgomery walked slowly. She'd still had no success finding a job. The walk seemed endless, but finally she turned down Bleeker Street and was home at last. She climbed slowly up the front stairs of a small, four-story brownstone. Stopping for a minute, she stared down at the scarred front door, remembering the first time she had seen it, the first time she had fit her shiny key into the lock and opened it. Today, the key felt heavy in her hand as she moved to unlock it. Once inside the vestibule, she saw that the tiny battered mail box was bursting with mail. After turning the small key in the lock she tugged at the crumpled letters, finally managing to get them out. She didn't recognize the handwriting on most of them, or the return addresses, but that was no surprise.

Taking a deep breath, Jennifer began to climb the steep, narrow stairs to her apartment.

"Jennifer? Is that you?"

Jennifer saw one of the apartment doors crack open to reveal Mrs. Maruzelli peering out at her. At ninety-two, she had lived in the small apartment house for over sixty years. Jennifer stopped and gazed down at the woman's careworn face.

"Yes, Mrs. Maruzelli, it's me." Jennifer attempted to smile. "How are you?"

"Okay, okay," Mrs. Maruzelli nodded quickly. Jennifer tried to move on before the old woman could ask her the next question, but she was too late.

"And how's that handsome man of yours?"

Jennifer sighed softly. Every day, it went the same way. Mrs. Maruzelli's daughter-in-law had explained that, although the old woman could remember the most exact details of events that had happened forty years before, she often forgot what had happened only yesterday. For just over the past four months she still asked Jennifer this same question every day. Jennifer tried to keep her voice controlled and even.

"Fine, Mrs. Maruzelli. He's just fine."

"Good. Good. See you later."

Jennifer waited until she heard the old woman snap the two safety locks in place, and then continued up the stairs. She wondered if she would ever be able to answer Mrs. Maruzelli's inevitable question without the familiar pain clutching at her heart.

Finally, she reached her apartment door and turned the key in the ancient lock. The door swung open with a creak of rusty hinges. The two tiny rooms were neat and quiet.

Putting down her shoulderbag she glanced quickly through the mail. So many bills—and more condolence cards. They kept coming, and the names those of the same people who had, such a short time before, sent wedding gifts.

Moving toward the bed, she kicked off her shoes and stretched her slender body down on the worn, patchwork quilt. Without meaning to, she stretched a thin arm across the bed to his side.

Terry.

She could still hardly believe it. Four months ago, his warm, strong arms had held her close to him in this bed. They had laughed and drunk wine out of paper cups and been helplessly in love. She could see him now, sitting crosslegged on the lumpy bed, playing his guitar and singing to her. And now, she would never hear him sing again.

Jennifer closed her eyes and tried to relax. She had spent the long day looking for a job. With Terry gone, she would soon have to find some way to pay the rent. She had to find a job—and fast.

The phone rang shrilly, piercing the stillness. For a minute, she considered not answering it. It would be her mother, or some other consoling voice. The phone continued ringing. She reached for it.

"Jennifer?"

"Yes?"

"It's David."

David. Terry's father. Terry had had David's eyes. Jennifer smiled in spite of herself.

"Hi."

"How are you doing?"

"Okay."

"Any luck with a job?"

9

"No." She felt the tears welling up inside her. "No," she repeated, trying to keep her voice firm. "Not yet." All those interviews and questions, the nice woman at the employment agency explaining that, with the economy in its present state, jobs were scarce and with her limited experience . . . .

"Well, listen," David's voice sounded hurried, "I had an idea—I have a friend who's the head of the news department at International Broadcast Systems and he told me at lunch that he's looking for some help and I told him I knew someone."

Jennifer stared up at the crack in the ceiling above her. News department? What was he talking about?

David continued. "He told me he needed another person in his department at an entry level position, production assistant I think he called it, and when I told him about you he was interested."

David was talking rapidly as if he was afraid she would interrupt. Production assistant in a television station? Her only job experience had been working in the college library and helping out in a daycare center. And then, when Terry asked her to marry him, she had not wanted to look for a job. She and Terry both loved children, and they wanted to start a family immediately. Involuntarily, Jennifer placed a hand over her flat stomach. She had wanted a baby so desperately, but Terry had died before . . . .

"Jennifer?" David asked. "Did you hear what I said?"

"Yes, but . . . I don't know anything about television news," she stammered. "And . . ."

"I know," David interjected smoothly, "but I told him you were bright and willing to learn and he agreed to give you an interview."

"Yes, but I—"

"And, anyway," David seemed to take a deep breath, "He owes me a favor."

So that was it. She was going to get a job interview because David knew someone. Jennifer passed a hand over her eyes. She had wanted to get a job on her own, to do something for herself to find a job and begin to pull her life back together. Her father had taken care of her until she was eighteen when he died of a heart attack. Then she had met Terry and he had always been strong and protective. Without question, she let him make all the decisions about the apartment, their finances, their plans for the future. When he died, she suddenly realized that she had depended on him for everything. She had never had to rely on herself, on her own judgment—there had always been someone else, some strong man around to take care of her. And now, here was David offering to help her, because Terry couldn't anymore.

How could she let him? Just once, she had to stand on her own two feet. She took a breath to turn down his offer and her eyes fell on the stack of unpaid bills on the bedside table. The last four months rent and living expenses had taken most of their savings. Thank goodness Terry's insurance covered the funeral—though just barely. The employment agencies had not sent her on a single interview. She quickly thought over what David had said. The news department. She knew nothing about television production or news, but David had said it was an "entry level" position, and she was more than willing to learn.

David's voice broke into her reverie. "He said you can go in and see him tomorrow. What do you think?"

"Of course," Jennifer said evenly, surprised at the calm, sure sound of her voice. David told her where and when to report and she scribbled the information down on a scrap of paper.

"Justin Bradley, International Broadcast Systems, One Lincoln Plaza, at noon sharp," she repeated. "David . . . thank you." She smiled. "I really appreciate it."

"Sure thing, honey. Let me know how it goes."

She hung up the phone slowly. Dear David . . . so kind, so generous—and with Terry's eyes.

No . . . she stopped her thoughts instantly. She couldn't think about him now. Pulling herself up off the bed, she moved quickly across the room to the small refrigerator, which was wedged beneath a makeshift counter Terry had built out of pine slabs and bricks. Snapping the top off a can of diet soda, she looked down at the scrap of paper clutched in her hand. Justin Bradley. She could imagine what he would look like. Silver hair, a three piece suit. She hoped he liked her. She needed this job.

The next day dawned warm and sunny. Jennifer opened her eyes and yawned, stretching slowly in the big double bed. Sometimes, before she came fully awake, she would imagine that the dream had come true, that she was a married woman, that Terry was already up and had left for work. But try as she might she could not hold the image. The dream faded, leaving her alone. Alone in the bed she had never shared with the man she loved.

No, she told herself desperately—it couldn't be true. After all, the wedding had been picture-perfect, had gone exactly as planned. She and Terry had been married in New Jersey on Christmas Eve in a candlelight ceremony. The four bridesmaids had worn green velvet dresses and carried bouquets of mistletoe and baby's breath. The church had been decorated with fir boughs and she could still remember the warm, woodsy smell.

And the reception. Terry's band had played and everyone had danced and laughed together. And then, at midnight, Terry had whispered that he had a surprise for her. Crossing to the bandstand, he'd taken the microphone in his hand and begun to sing "Brown-Eyed Lady," the song he had written for her. He had looked deeply into her eyes and there had been no one else in the room except the two of them, together.

Jennifer felt the tears welling up behind her eyelids. She would never forget the sound of his voice singing to her. Then, after a shower of rice and good wishes, they drove away from the reception in Terry's old Volkswagen and headed back to New York City. They were going to spend their honeymoon in their own small, warm apartment. Terry told her he especially want to spend their wedding night in the home—and the bed—where they would live as man and wife.

Jennifer shivered, shutting her eyes against the memories. The small car had started across the ice-covered George Washington Bridge. Terry was driving and she asked him to sing the song again, the one he had written for her. He was singing softly, the tiny car warm against the freezing winds. Suddenly, a car came careening out of the toll booths on the Manhattan side of the bridge. It skidded on the ice and smashed into the Volkswagen with a squeal of rubber and crash of splintering glass. Terry had been killed instantly.

Jennifer felt the tears streaming down her cheeks. For the hundredth time since that nightmare moment, she wished with all her heart that she had died with him. It was not fair that she had barely been injured, but had lost the only man she had ever loved.

The morning sun streamed into the room as Jennifer turned her head to stare at their wedding picture. It had been taken only moments before that sound . . . the screeching brakes . . . her own screaming. . . .

Don't think about that now! Jennifer sat up quickly and brushed the tears from her face. Think about today, the interview, meeting Mr. Justin Bradley and convincing him you can be the best— what was it David said?—the best production assistant International Broadcast Systems has ever had.

Swinging her legs down she stood up quickly, her long cotton nightgown clinging to her thin frame. Moving to the bureau, she picked up her brush and pulled it through her hair in long, even strokes. Peering into the cloudy mirror, she wiped the tear away and took a hard look at herself.

Her eyes were large and brown, tipped with long black lashes. Her hair, which fell to her shoulders, was wavy and thick and a honey yellow color. She'd lost weight in the last months, her body slender beneath the flowing nightgown. Dark smudges circled her eyes. Too many tears and not enough sleep, she mused. Sighing softly, she replaced the brush. A touch of makeup would help.

She showered quickly in her tiny bathroom and wrapped herself in a thick, soft towel. Snatching up the piece of paper, she read the address again, One Lincoln Plaza. She'd take the subway uptown. She didn't want to be late. She had plenty of time.

Jennifer pushed back the curtain that served as a closet door and surveyed her wardrobe. Even before she pushed through the nearly empty hangers, she knew she had only one dress suitable to wear to a job interview with the news director of International Broadcast Systems. With a determined effort, she reached to the back of the closet and pulled out a soft, blue dress gathered at the waist and neck in a peasant style. Her breath caught at the sight of it. She had not worn it since the funeral. She had pushed it to the back of the closet, not wanting to remember the day Terry had bought it for her.

Jennifer held the soft dress to her face and closed her eyes. All those sad faces at the funeral. So many people she hadn't known. And perhaps the saddest picture of all, Terry's musician friends, their long hair combed, their tall lean bodies dressed in ill-fitting suits and frayed ties, touching her hand and telling her the band had not played again since the night Terry died.

Jennifer's eyes flew open suddenly and she stared at the small clock on the bedside table. Almost ten-thirty! She couldn't be late. Taking a deep breath, she took the dress off the hanger. It would bring good luck. She knew it.

Smoothing her hair once more, Jennifer looked into the mirror and stood on tiptoe to see the full picture. Her eyes seemed huge in her small, pale face. Her hair, parted in the middle and pulled back on each side with the combs Terry had given her for her last birthday, was clean and shining. A touch of lipstick had made her mouth look brighter and her face less sad. The blue dress accentuated her small waist. She slipped her feet into her only pair of high heeled sandals and smiled slightly into the mirror. Well, she thought looking critically at her reflection, Mr. Justin Bradley of International Broadcast Systems, here I come.

Two

Justin Bradley's office was open and Jennifer could see him standing with his back to her looking out a huge floor to ceiling window. Dazzling sunlight filled the room, shining in on the carpet, walls and furniture. The dramatic effect was heightened by the fact that the entire office was decorated in beige and white. Justin stood behind a massive desk which consisted of a six-foot by five-foot glass rectangle perched on thin chrome legs. The design of the desk gave the illusion that all the papers, books and pencils which cluttered its surface were suspended in mid air. Jennifer moved hesitantly across the thick, shag carpeting and lowered herself into a chair, the only space in the room not covered with papers. Justin continued to talk rapidly into the phone.

"I know, but there's no way we can do a documentary like that for under five hundred thousand. That's cheap for an hour's programming, and, of course, they'll air it again. There's a lot of interest now—and it can always be sold to syndication and they'll get their money back down the line . . . ."

Justin had not turned when she entered the room and Jennifer wondered nervously whether he was aware she was sitting in front of his desk, listening in on his conversation. She clutched her shoulder-bag tightly and watched Justin pace up and down in front of the spectacular view of Lincoln Center. She smiled to herself, remembering what she had imagined Justin Bradley would look like. A silver haired man in a three-piece suit indeed! Her mental picture of the head of International Broadcast Systems news department couldn't have been farther from the truth.

Justin Bradley towered above her as she looked up at him from her seated position. His broad shoulders and powerful neck were visible beneath the thin beige suede of his jacket. His hair was dark and curled down softly to his collar. As he moved in front of the window, Jennifer watched his profile silhouetted against the sunlight. His jaw was proud and strong. He held the phone clenched in his powerful looking fist. His deep, rich voice continued.

"I know, I know . . . well, see what you can do. If I cut out a few locations, it's possible to bring it in under a million, but I'd rather budget high and come in under it than go way over—okay. I appreciate it."

Turning smoothly, he placed the receiver back on the phone console and hurriedly scribbled a few notes on a legal pad.

"There!" He threw down a pencil and stacked a pile of papers together quickly. He still had not looked at her.

"Now . . ." He looked up and smiled. Jennifer smiled back. Before he could say anything, she heard her own voice filling the silence.

"Hello. I'm Jennifer Montgomery. My father-in-law, David, spoke to you about me." She was relieved at how strong and sure her voice sounded. "I really appreciate your giving me this job interview. I don't have any experience in television news but I know I can learn, and I . . ." her voice wavered. Justin Bradley had stopped smiling. His face was somehow changing before her eyes, the smile disappearing. He looked gray beneath his tan. What had she said? She tried again.

"I'm very willing to learn, to work hard—I can pick things up quickly, if someone just shows me. I can . . . I will . . ."

He was staring at her, simply staring. His smile was gone. His eyes, a piercing blue, looked stunned and lifeless. Jennifer stopped talking and the two stared at each other in silence. Faintly, Jennifer could hear the office sounds coming in from the open door. She longed to go back outside, back to the receptionist's desk and come in and start all over again. She wanted to flee from the glaring sunlight and the cold blue eyes that stared at her steadily. What had she said to make him look at her like that? Was he angry? But how could he be angry with her? She was only telling him the truth. David had told him that she'd had no experience in news, and she had said she was willing to learn. She heard her voice continuing in a frightened attempt to fill the silence.

"Of course . . . I understand if you're not willing to teach me, I mean, I would understand if you didn't want to take the time . . ." Her voice trailed off. He didn't look as if he was breathing. Suddenly, the phone rang, shattering the silence. Jennifer jumped involuntarily at the sound. Justin made no move to pick it up.

Jennifer clutched her shoulderbag and moved to the edge of her chair. She had to get out of there, she thought desperately. This had all been a terrible mistake.

The phone rang and rang, but Justin Bradley did not appear to hear it. He sat immobile, his strong hands gripping the desk for support. He had not moved or spoken since he'd first looked into her eyes. The phone rang on. Suddenly, shaking himself, he grabbed the receiver.

"No calls!" he said angrily and slammed it down with such force the desk shook and a pile of papers fluttered to the carpet.

Jennifer found herself on her feet, backing hastily out of the sunlit office.

"Mr. Bradley, I really thank you for seeing me . . . I'm sorry if anything I've said has upset you. I . . ." Her heel caught in the thick shag carpeting and she stumbled backward. Somehow she remained standing.

"Goodbye Mr. Bradley." She turned quickly hurrying toward the door. Pain and confusion made the room swirl about her.

"Please—"Justin's voice stopped her. He had pulled himself up out of his chair. Jennifer stood uncertainly, mesmerized by the look in his eyes.

He moved slowly around the massive desk to where she stood in the center of the room. He shook his head slightly, as if to clear it, and attempted to smile. Standing in front of her, he reached up and placed his hands on her shoulders and looked deeply into her eyes.

"Jennifer," he said, his voice growing stronger, "you said your name was Jennifer . . ."

Jennifer could feel his warm hands through the thin fabric of her dress. The scent of his cologne wafted over her as she looked up into his ruggedly handsome face.

"Jennifer," he continued, "David has told me a lot about you and I am very happy to meet you. When you first walked in—for a moment I . . . well," he shrugged.

Jennifer was barely hearing his words. She could feel the weight of his strong hands on her shoulders. She didn't breathe, but held herself motionless. He moved his hands slightly and for one insane moment she thought he was going to lower his mouth to hers and kiss her. Somewhere a phone rang and a typewriter clacked busily. His eyes never left her face. His hands dropped to his side.

"The hours are long and the pay is low . . ." He seemed to be making an effort to keep his voice even and controlled. "But . . . I think you'll enjoy working with us."

Jennifer's heart leapt. Working—He was giving her the job? He had heard what she'd been telling him and had decided to give her a chance! Before she could thank him, he pushed the intercom button on his desk, his manner suddenly brisk and businesslike.

"Diana," his voice was firm and strong, "Please send Lilly in here."

He slowly lowered himself into the chrome and leather chair and placed his head in his hands, pulling his fingers through the thick, wavy hair. Looking up, he smiled at Jennifer.

"Lilly will show you around the office."

As if on cue, a young woman in tight-fitting jeans and a satin baseball jacket walked through the door.

"Lilly," Justin's voice took on a warm tone, "this is Jennifer. She's the new production assistant in news. Will you show her around please?"

Lilly snapped her bubble gum and looked at him strangely, then shrugged.

"Sure." Turning to Jennifer, she smiled and held out her hand. "Welcome aboard, you'll love it here." Jennifer smiled back and followed her out of the office. Lilly seemed like a nice, normal person. At least someone was.

"Boy, that was weird," Lilly stopped to fill a tiny paper cup with water at the water cooler.

"What was?" Jennifer asked.

"Justin always shows new people around himself. You know, makes a new employee feel welcome, the personal touch . . ." She peered at Jennifer over the rim of her cup. "He seemed to be in a really strange mood. I've never seen him look like that." Her gum snapped and she shrugged slightly. "Oh well, I guess he's got a lot on his mind."

Jennifer followed Lilly through the thickly carpeted halls.

Why hadn't Justin wanted to show her around the office? And why had he stared at her with that strange look in his eyes? Maybe he felt pressured to give her the job because of his friendship with David.

But—in that case—he might have been abrupt with her, but he hadn't been. No, it was something else . . .

"Jennifer?" Lilly touched her on the arm. "Wow, Justin isn't the only one who's spaced today." She looked closely at Jennifer's vacant expression. "Come *on* . . . Boy," she said, shaking her head. "What is it with everyone around here, is it a full moon or something?"

With an effort Jennifer turned to her and smiled. "No, it's just new-on-the-job jitters," she explained, unable to understand either Justin's attitude—or her own.

Two hours later, Jennifer was back on Broadway, and, for the first time since Terry's death, the world was looking bright and beautiful again. Stopping at the first phone booth she could find, she dropped a dime into the slot and dialed David's number. A secretary answered and put her call right through.

"How did it go?" David asked anxiously.

"Great!" Jennifer couldn't keep the excitement out of her voice. "I got the job!"

"Congratulations!" He sounded very pleased.

"I owe it all to you!"

"No way." David's voice was instantly serious. "I suggested you to Justin, but you got this job on the strength of your job interview, on his meeting you and liking what you had to say for yourself. You don't owe me anything."

Jennifer gripped the phone receiver tightly. On the strength of her job interview! She could imagine

David's face if he had witnessed the "job interview" in Justin Bradley's office.

David's voice continued, " . . . just have a good time and enjoy yourself," his voice lowered slightly, "you deserve it."

"Thanks, David."

"Jen?"

"Yes?"

"What did you think of Justin? Great guy, right?" Jennifer took a deep breath. She couldn't tell him. Justin was his friend. How could she possibly describe the way he had reacted when he first saw her in his office or tell him that Justin had barely spoken to her?

"Well, what did you think? He's one of the nicest men I know. A little quiet sometimes, but very friendly and dedicated to his work."

Nice? Jennifer thought glumly. Were they talking about the same man?

"Jennifer? Are you still there?"

Whatever had happened between her and Justin Bradley, it was her problem. David need never know. She would work it out.

"Yes, I'm here. Yes, Mr. Bradley was definitely the most, uh, interesting man I've met in a long time."

"He's the best," David agreed heartily. "Now listen, I have to go, but I'll take you to lunch one day when you get into the routine."

"Thank you, I'd like that."

"Good-bye, honey."

"Good-bye."

Jennifer could feel the sun warming the phone booth as she replaced the receiver slowly.

Nice? Friendly? That was not the word she would have used to describe Justin Bradley, but . . . She squared her shoulders and marched out of the phone booth. He had hired her and she would show him. She'd work hard and learn fast and prove to him she'd be an important addition to his staff. She wasn't just David Montgomery's daughter-in-law, but a woman on her own, who needed this job and would make it a success.

Three

The next few weeks flew by in a blur of activity. Jennifer learned quickly and Lilly and the others on the news production staff were eager to help her. On the morning of her first day, Jennifer had been assigned a cubbyhole of an office next to Lilly's and the two became instant friends.

A year older than Jennifer, Lilly had worked in television production since she quit high school to become a "go-fer" on a local midwest television station. A "go-fer," as Jennifer soon learned, was the person on a television production staff who had to "go-fer" coffee and cigarettes and run the endless errands that were essential to the smooth running of a television show. Lilly had been with Independent Broadcast News for two years and the office grapevine was alive with the news that she was soon to be promoted to associate producer of the Ten P.M. *Nightly News.*

Jennifer found herself watching Lilly closely, listening to her on the phone, trying to imitate Lilly's confident, aggressive style. As Jennifer began to understand the extent of her new responsibilities as

a production assistant, she became even more determined to learn everything about her new job as
quickly as possible. She worked late every night often
staying to watch Lilly or one of the other production
assistants work the nightly live news broadcast. Fascinated by the different elements that went into a
successful show, she asked what seemed to her to be
hundreds of questions and scribbled notes frantically on long yellow legal pads.

Jennifer had not seen Justin Bradley since that
first day in his office. Lilly had mentioned offhandedly that Justin had left the morning following Jennifer's job interview to meet a crew filming in Europe.

"Strange," Lilly had leaned against the thin parti-
tion of Jennifer's makeshift office. "I made Justin's
plane reservations myself and he wasn't due on the
site for a week. The next thing I know, he's changed
his reservations and he leaves the next day. That's
not like him at all . . ."

Strange . . . Jennifer felt a cold fear clutch at her
heart. He had left suddenly the day after he had hired
her. Why? Don't be foolish, she cautioned herself.
Justin had to leave earlier than he had planned, and
just didn't have a chance to tell Lilly. His sudden de-
parture had nothing to do with her. But, even as she
repeated these words over and over in her mind, she
could not make herself believe them.

According to the huge master schedule pasted on
the wall of Lilly's office, Justin was not due back from
location for another five weeks. Jennifer drew a red
magic marker line through those five weeks on her
desk calendar. Five weeks to master the complexities
of her new job. She would do it. When Justin re-

turned she would be ready to show him that she was capable and efficient and worthy of her place on the news staff.

The days settled into a hectic pattern of production meetings, script revisions and fast breaking news stories. Every day's activities culminated in the nightly live news broadcast. The production assistants took turns working late one night a week during the show, helping the producer, associate producer and stage manager keep everything running smoothly. After a month on the staff, Jennifer was called into the office of the show's associate producer, Ray Tomara.

"I'd like to put you down for the live broadcast Thursday night," Ray told her in a matter-of-fact tone. He looked at her closely. "Do you think you're ready?"

Thursday night! Jennifer's heart skipped a beat and then steadied as she looked into Ray's friendly face. Suddenly a phrase from an old song crossed her mind—it's now or never.

She smiled back at him. "Yes, I'm ready."

"Good." He picked up the show's production schedule and scribbled "Jennifer Montgomery" on the Thursday night staff roster. She was to report to the office at three o'clock and work through the evening's show until eleven-thirty.

"And don't worry!" he laughed at her worried face. "You've learned everything you need to know. You'll do fine." Jennifer nodded nervously, then turned to leave Ray's cluttered office.

"Oh, and Jennifer?" Ray's voice made her stop and turn back.

"What?"

"Tell your mother that your name will be on the credit crawl after Thursday's show. Relatives get a big kick out of that stuff."

Jennifer stared at him and then her face lit with a big smile.

"Do you mean it?" She asked him quickly.

Ray smiled at her warmly. "Yes, of course I mean it. You've earned it."

Jennifer could barely conceal her excitement. Thursday night her name would appear in the credits with the rest of the *Nightly News* staff. Ray had said she was ready to take on the night shift. She'd worked hard and knew she would have nothing to worry about. Only two things saddened her. The first was that Terry was not alive to share this moment with her. He would have been so proud of her. She felt the familiar tears begin to well up inside her and with a determined effort forced herself not to think about him. Instead, she turned her thoughts to her second disappointment. Mr. Justin Bradley would not be witness to her new success. He would not be in the studio to see how professionally she could handle herself during the live broadcast.

Oh well, she smiled once more as she left Ray's office. Justin would be back soon enough and Thursday night would be her first chance to show them all that they had taught her well. She wouldn't disappoint them.

From her bed Jennifer noted that Thursday morning was cloudy with a fine misty rain. She stretched luxuriously as she remembered that she didn't have to get up and fight the rush hour crowds to work, that she had most of the day to herself and tonight, tonight she would be working on a live television show.

Actually, when she thought about it, she was grateful that Justin Bradley was out of town. This first night would give her a chance to try her wings, to get an idea of what working the show was like. By the time he got back from location, she would be poised and confident. She knew he would be pleased with her progress.

At least she hoped so, she thought as she stretched her arms over her head. Lately, she had been able to wake up and not immediately think of Terry. Maybe it was her demanding schedule, but, she had to admit to herself, her new exciting job made it easier not to miss him so much.

Not that she was forgetting him! She sat up suddenly and pulled their wedding picture off the bedside table and held it to her chest. She would never forget the happy days they had spent together, she swore to herself—never!

Jennifer dressed carefully for her first night on the News show, her first paycheck having gone toward some new clothes. When she finished dressing, she peered into the mirror and admired the effect. A pair of brand new designer jeans, short leather boots, a bright pink T-shirt that brought out the warm tone of her skin, and, her most precious new possession, a silver satin baseball jacket, just like Lilly's, with "Nightly News" emblazoned on the back. Each member of the news team was awarded a jacket when promoted to working the live show.

Ray Tomara was glad to see her. There had been some late breaking developments in the Middle East crisis and the police had just received word that a world-renowned New York City heiress had been kidnapped. All the copy for the night's news, the running order for the show, the pre-taped segments, everything had to be changed.

For the next five hours, Jennifer worked side by side with Ray, running back and forth between the copy room, the studio and the production office. At eight-thirty, Ray pushed himself back from his desk and stood wearily.

"O.K., that's it. We're as ready as we'll ever be." He took a quick look at his watch. "Eight-thirty! Wow! I'll stand by here, why don't you run down and grab a sandwich. I'll need you back here by nine." He swiveled his head slowly, trying to relieve the tension in his neck, then he smiled at the concern on her face.

"Don't worry about me. It comes with the job. Oh, and, by the way," he added softly. "You're doing great."

Jennifer grabbed her bag and smiled back at him as she pushed the door open onto the deserted halls of International Broadcast Systems. Some of the production staff found it eerie to work in the empty offices without the familiar faces, the constant clack of typewriters, the ringing phones, but Jennifer found it peaceful and somehow, comforting. The large windows reflected a darkened city sparkling with tiny lights, the soft carpet and intense quiet made the office seem like a completely different place than the efficient news station it was during the day.

Pushing the button for the elevator, Jennifer automatically grabbed her brush from her shoulderbag and pulled it through her hair. Suddenly, she stopped with the brush poised in mid air. She remembered Ray's face when he had watched her brushing her long, thick hair.

"You don't have to bother brushing your hair all the time," he'd told her smiling, "You look sensational."

Ray. She had worked with Ray for over a month and yet she had never really thought of him as anything but a friendly man who was easy to work with. He was tall and slender with warm, laughing eyes and a ready smile. Lilly had made a point of telling her that Ray was single. But—Jennifer suddenly admitted to herself—since Terry's death, dating or meeting other men had been the last thing on her mind. She knew she was looking better than she had in months. She'd gained back enough weight to take the pinched look out of her face and the dark circles had disappeared from beneath her eyes. And yet, no one in the office had asked her out for a date.

She shook her head thoughtfully. The men in the office had been kind and friendly to her, but that was all. And yet, maybe it was because she seemed reluctant to get to know them any better. She knew nothing about Ray, how long he'd been at International Broadcast Systems, what his interests were. Could it be that she had shut off that part of her life so completely that she couldn't bring herself to get close to any other man? Could she have been hurt so deeply by Terry's death, that she couldn't risk that kind of pain again?

Jennifer pushed impatiently at the elevator button. The numbers above the elevator door indicated it was still on the ground floor.

But, she had to admit to herself, it wasn't exactly true that she hadn't thought about any other man since Terry's death. Since the day she had walked into his office, the image of Justin Bradley haunted her. Every day, coming into work, she would glance secretly into his office, hoping he had returned from Europe. She couldn't deny that she was eager to see him again.

Justin Bradley, exhausted after three weeks of location shooting, cursed the ponderous elevator as it moved slowly toward the sixteenth floor. The late night visit to the office to retrieve his mail and check on the night's broadcast was important, but he was anxious to get it over with. He watched impatiently as the lights above the elevator door lit slowly with each approaching floor, and then they finally opened.

Carrying a heavy suitcase in each hand, Justin hurried forward before Jennifer could say a word, and collided solidly with her soft body. She stumbled backward. Dropping his bags in an immediate reflex action, Justin reached out to hold her and stop her fall. His strong arms held her firmly. Gasping, Jennifer looked up into the blue eyes she had not seen for such a long time. His face was so close to hers, she could feel his breath on her lips. His eyes were lined with fatigue, circled with deep shadows. But as he stared down into her upturned face, she saw something else held in those deep blue eyes, something she had not seen before.

He made no move to remove his arms but slowly . . . so slowly . . . closed them around her, pulling her to him. She felt the strength of his chest as she was crushed against him. For a long moment he gazed into her eyes before he lowered his head slightly and pressed his mouth over hers.

Suddenly it seemed as if the room was spinning, the world was reeling, and the only thing certain was the strength of his warm arms around her and the mouth that possessed hers. Without thinking, Jennifer moved her arms up to encircle his neck . . .

Slowly, Justin released her. They stood breathlessly facing each other.

Jennifer's mind raced in confusion. His arms had closed around her and she had responded instinctively to the warmth of his touch. It had been so long . . . so long since strong arms had held her close, so long since warm lips caressed her . . .

She could not move or speak. She looked into Justin's eyes, searching their depths for an answer to the turmoil in her heart. Her breath caught at the sadness etched in his face.

Gently, he pushed her away from him and reached for his scattered luggage. Stopping suddenly, he turned back and looked into her eyes.

"I'm sorry . . ." he said softly. "I'm very—sorry."

Jennifer could not think, could feel nothing but the painful beating of her heart. In one motion, Justin gathered up his bags and was striding away from her, disappearing down the empty hall, leaving her standing alone, feeling a cold chill envelop her where once his warm arms had been.

* * *

Jennifer pushed the heavy security door of the studio, and hurried past the guard who smiled at her. Clutching a clipboard with the script for that night's show, she tried to still her rapid breathing and concentrate on the job ahead. She placed a cool hand on her burning cheek and shut her eyes, trying to get control of herself. Justin Bradley or no Justin Bradley, she reminded herself, tonight is my first chance at working on a live television show and everything had to go smoothly.

The technical crew was milling around the newsroom set, positioning cameras and adjusting lights. Jennifer took a deep breath and squared her shoulders. Ray. She had to find Ray. She threaded her way through the crowded studio floor until she encountered him talking to the show's director, Sam Lewis.

"Hi," Ray looked at Jennifer's flushed face and smiled. "You all set?"

Jennifer nodded hurriedly. Ray looked at her closely for a moment, then shrugged and moved off toward the control room. She had absent-mindedly walked in front of one of the cameras. Her image was transmitted through the cameras to one of the large television monitors positioned on the floor. She stared at herself. Her hair was disheveled, her eyes bright. She tried desperately to relax. I will think about Justin later, she told herself sternly, later, when it's quiet and she could be alone. Now was the time to work.

Erica King, the anchorwoman for the *Nightly News* walked onto the set, closely accompanied by

Carlo, her hairdresser and Tania, the makeup artist. Erica settled herself regally in her accustomed leather and chrome chair behind the wide circular desk which was the main feature of the set. Pursing her lips, she turned to Tania who took a thin bright lipstick from a cosmetics bag and brushed at Erica's lips with short, expert strokes.

"Jennifer?"

Erica's rich, husky voice cut through the noise in the studio. Jennifer hurried quickly to her side.

The show's producers had designed the *Nightly News* set to look like a working newsroom. Colored telephones were strewn across the shiny wood surface of the circular desk. Jennifer knew, as did the rest of the crew, that these phones were only "props," that the cords which curled away from them in every direction hung uselessly over the back of the desk. Three more leather and chrome chairs were placed next to Monica's around the desk. These would soon be filled with the rest of the show's staff of reporters. Behind the desk was a large piece of canvas designed to look like a window reflecting the Manhattan skyline as it looked at ten P.M. The first day she had walked into the studio Jennifer had recognized the view. It was an exact duplicate of the window in Justin Bradley's office.

Jennifer remembered how she and Terry had sat and watched the *Nightly News* every evening. He had been especially impressed with Erica King's celebrity interviews. With ease and assurance, she asked precise, timely questions of heads of state, presidents, kings. With her dark head bent toward her guest, she would listen carefully to the complex answer. And when they replied to one of her questions with what might seem to be a surprising answer, she was never at a loss for words. Without hesitation, the next question flowed expertly out of her glistening lips. Terry had considered her a genius. In her first days at the news station, Jennifer had discovered that Erica's carefully worded questions were whispered to her by a news expert sitting in the control room through a tiny earphone almost hidden in her mass of thick brown hair. When Erica gave an interview on location, the expert would stand close by, giving her the exact phrasing for the next question via a small hidden microphone. Amazed, Jennifer realized that, in many cases, Erica King, the beautiful, poised anchorwoman for the *Nightly News*, would be at a loss for words without her expert's advice.

"Will you check this script for me?" she asked Jennifer quietly. "I don't think the pages are in order."

Jennifer always marveled at the sound of Erica's voice. Somehow, no matter what story she was relating, bomb threats, assasination attempts, war, hijackings, death, her smooth voice seemed to make them seem less frightening. Jennifer smiled back, as she realized that the charm of this magnetic voice was making her relax a little too.

She quickly checked the script and handed it back.

"This is your first show isn't it?" Erica attempted to turn toward Jennifer while Carol and Tania fluttered around her head.

"Yes . . ." Jennifer tried to make her voice sound calm and relaxed.

"Well, you'll have no problem," Erica assured her. "Will you tell Jerry the lights feel a bit harsh?"

"Sure," Jennifer hurried off to find the lighting director. Another revelation. All of the studio lights which show down on Erica's head were covered with a pink "gel," a piece of thin transparent plastic that softened the light, made her complexion warmer. Other lights, directed up at her face from a lower position, reduced the wrinkles around her eyes. Erica King insisted that these lights always be correctly in place.

Rushing about, Jennifer thought occasionally about Justin, remembering the feel of his warm arms around her and the compelling demands of his mouth on hers. It had happened so fast. But she knew, as soon as he had kissed her, that she wanted him to, had wanted to feel his touch from the moment they had met. And now that it had happened, all she wanted was to feel him kiss her again.

But, would he? The sadness in his eyes. The sound of his voice when he had said he was sorry. Sorry for what? And that look in his eyes, strange and empty and sad. Why? Why did he look at her like that? For everyone else he had a ready smile, a warmth that everyone could feel. But when he had kissed her, Jennifer suddenly smiled to herself, there had been nothing remote in that. She had felt the passion stirring in him as his mouth moved on hers. She had not imagined it. It was real.

"Jennifer?" Ray's voice cut into her thoughts. She turned quickly to find him standing beside her. "We go on the air in fifteen minutes, is everything ready?"

Jennifer smiled at him assuredly. "All ready."

"Good and good luck." Jennifer watched Ray hurry back to the control room. Fifteen minutes to air!

There were a hundred things still to do. Thoughts of Justin would have to wait.

"Ten seconds . . ." Carl Montera, the show's stage manager said loudly. He began to count off in a commanding tone. "7–6–5–4 . . ." He pointed at Erica, who lifted her dark head and looked directly into the camera poised in front of her. In a voice known to millions of television viewers, she said confidently: "Good evening. This is the Ten P.M. Nightly News. I'm Erica King."

Jennifer heard the rich, deep voice continue, calmly outlining the evening's headlining news stories. Erica then introduced her co-anchorman Steve Harrington. Steve smiled at her and complimented Erica on her beautiful hand-embroidered blouse. This was what Lilly called "carefully rehearsed spontaneity." The show's producers wanted their audience to think that, as Erica and Steve opened the show, they were merely stopping in the midst of a hectic day in the newsroom to relate the news to an anxiously waiting public to whom they wanted to give the impression that they had just finished compiling their news stories seconds before the show went on the air. The truth, as Jennifer soon learned, was that Erica and Steve saw the script for the evening's show only minutes before air time.

Erica thanked Steve prettily and asked about his vacation in Aspen. The producers also wanted the news staff, Erica, Steve, Spencer Jones, the weatherman and Linda Cornell, the sports announcer, to engage in friendly banter throughout the course of the show. They wanted their audience to hear the news in a relaxed atmosphere and wanted the staff to give the impression they were a big happy "family." But, as Lilly explained to Jennifer, there were famous stories in television history of disastrous "ad libs," casual comments which had been well-meant by the news commentators but, telecast instantly around the country, were often misunderstood by the listening public. For this reason, the playful banter on the *Nightly News* was supplied by staff writers. Steve's and Erica's opening remarks had been carefully read off small blue cards concealed in their scripts.

Erica and Steve introduced the other members of the newsteam who reviewed the highlights of their upcoming reports. Erica said smoothly, "We'll be right back," and the show went to a commercial.

During this one minute break, Carlo fluttered around Erica's head and Steve reshuffled his papers. He was to open the show with the lead story on the Middle East crisis.

Jennifer stood between Carl and Janet Monteith, one of the shows news writers. Jennifer's most important function during the live broadcast was to monitor the teletype machines which provided constant updates on news stories around the world. If one of these stories broke during the show, the teletype machine would print the information instantly. Jennifer knew she was to tear the item off the printer and, if there was time before the broadcast ended, Janet would hastily write it up and hand it to Carl who would pass it on to Erica or Steve. Lilly had explained that sometimes news stories would come in just before "sign off." When this happened, the teletype printout was handed directly to Erica or Steve who related the news in his or her words.

I hope there's nothing out of the ordinary about tonight's show, Jennifer thought nervously. She only wanted the night's broadcast to be over, for everything to go smoothly and then, she could collapse in relief.

Spencer Jones was finishing his weather forecast and "throwing" the show to the sports announcer, Linda Cornell. No problems so far. Ray came out of the control room and caught Jennifer's eye. Raising a hand in an okay sign, he smiled. Jennifer smiled back. So far, so good!

"Jennifer!" Erica's voice was raised in alarm. The show was on a commerical break. Carl had just announced that there were thirty seconds to go until the show went back on the air. Erica's head had disappeared behind the circular desk and she was shuffling with papers. Jennifer hurried to her.

"I've dropped my script!" Erica snapped. The flimsy pages of the show's script were scattered across the floor. Jennifer got down on her knees and began to stack them into a pile. Carl's strong voice filled the studio.

"Ten seconds . . . 9–8–7 . . ." Jennifer tried to get up and get out from under the desk and back to her safe position. As she struggled with the rumpled pages Jennifer suddenly felt Erica's long fingernails grip her shoulder, firmly pushing her down behind the desk.

". . . 4–3 . . ." There was no time. She was trapped, huddled under the news desk as the show went back on the air.

Jennifer heard Steve's voice introducing the "On the Town" segment, a weekly special feature about one of New York City's famous restaurants. She listened as Steve asked Erica calmly about the decor of the restaurant featured on the upcoming report. Horrified, Jennifer looked down and realized she was holding the carefully written description of the gourmet restaurant in her hand. Above her, Erica faced the camera with no idea which restaurant was the subject of the pre-taped report.

Shutting her eyes, Jennifer heard Erica's husky voice begin without hesitation.

"Yes . . . thank you Steve . . . Tonight we visit one of New York City's most beautiful restaurants. It is famous throughout the world for its elegant cuisine and impeccable service. I think you'll really enjoy this special feature on this memorable restaurant."

"Rolling!" Carl said crisply. He meant that the pre-taped segment on "Le Cirque" was on the air. The studio had two minutes before they were back live.

Jennifer scrambled up from her cramped position and hurriedly straightened the script pages into proper numerical order.

Carl's voice, "Ready! 10 seconds . . . 9–8–7 . . ."

Erica gave Jennifer a calm smile as she took the script back and turned to face the camera.

". . . 3–2 . . ."

Jennifer hurried back to stand beside Ray who waited with a strained expression beside the script writer. As she ran to stand beside him, she began to feel her breath begin its even rhythm again.

Erica and Steve began the "wrap-up," summarizing the day's news headlines and teasing each other in carefully worded questions and answers about their personal plans for the upcoming weekend. Finally the show's theme music began. Carl lifted his hand over his head. Erica and Steve said "good night." Carl's hand fell. The camera lights went off. The show was over.

"Wow!" Ray turned to Jennifer and threw an arm around her shoulders. "That was close! This time you can tell your mother you really *were* on television, she just didn't see you."

Jennifer smiled up at him. She had made it. She hadn't panicked, hadn't rushed to her feet and gotten into the shot. Her face had not been transmitted across the country. Lilly had warned her that, no matter what happened, she must never get in front of the camera, must never be seen on the show. She had remembered Lilly's words. She'd done the right thing.

Ray squeezed her shoulders in a friendly hug and hurried back to the control room.

Watching him stride away, Jennifer allowed herself a satisfied smile. Suddenly, the smile froze on her face. Directly across from her, towering above the milling staff on the crowded studio floor, two cold blue eyes regarded her steadily. Her breath caught. She stared back into the handsome face. Their eyes held for a painful moment, and she was aware of no one else in the room, no sound. The cavernous space seemed empty except for her and him, suspended in time, held together by an electric force.

Abruptly, Justin Bradley turned and disappeared. The noise and confusion erupted around Jennifer's ears.

He was gone.

Jennifer and Lilly walked slowly around a huge table in the I.B.S. conference room, methodically compiling and stapling the scripts for the upcoming documentary shoot. Justin Bradley was taking Lilly and a technical crew to China to tape a ninety-minute television special. It was all anyone had talked about for weeks.

"Lilly . . ."

"Ummmm . . . ."

Jennifer hesitated before a stack of papers and tried to form her question carefully.

"Um . . . how well do you know Justin?" she asked, forcing her voice to sound relaxed and casual.

"Justin?" Lilly shrugged. "Well, I don't know—I've worked for him for almost two years. He's *great* to work for, a lot of fun and friendly . . ."

Jennifer looked at her closely. Fun and friendly— the same impression of him, basically, that David had. She shook her head as she slammed the stapler firmly. Why did he seem so different to her?

"I don't know too much about his personal life," Lilly continued, "except of course the latest hot news on the grapevine . . ." She pushed a lock of hair behind her ear and grinned mischievously.

"What's that?" Jennifer asked, trying to concentrate on counting the pile of papers in her hand.

"Justin and Erica are being 'seen about town' as they say in the society columns."

Jennifer felt her heart give an uneven thump. Justin and Erica King?

"Pretty neat, huh?" Lilly grinned and Jennifer managed a weak smile. "Justin is one of New York

City's most eligible bachelors. The word is he has never been married and with his money and those dark, mysterious eyes . . . it didn't take Erica long to get her claws into him."

Jennifer looked at her sharply.

"You don't like Erica very much do you?" she asked.

"Well. . . ." Lilly shrugged, "It's just a feeling I get about her. While so many people on the staff here are really nice, with her I get the impression that everything is somehow calculated . . ." Lilly's voice trailed off.

"But she's a very good anchorwoman," Jennifer protested in spite of herself.

"That's true," Lilly agreed, "Even though you'd think she was totally dependent on cue cards and microphones in her ear, she handles a lot of situations well—like when you were stuck under the desk with that description she needed. But . . ." she continued cheerfully, "Justin probably isn't too interested in what she has to *say* anyway, if you know what I mean . . . ."

Jennifer pressed her weight heavily down on the stapler, fastening the pages with a resounding crunch. Why should Lilly's revelations have such an effect on her? she asked herself angrily. Erica *was* poised and sophisticated and beautiful. She and Justin made a very handsome couple. But, even as these thoughts went through her mind, she felt a wave of jealousy engulfing her. Unable to dispell the memory of Justin's strong arms pulling her toward him, she wanted so much to feel again the burning caress of his lips on hers. But now that would not happen. Justin obviously was involved with Erica.

"All set?" Lilly asked brightly as she stapled the last script.

Jennifer turned, a small sigh escaping her.

"Yes . . ." she replied hollowly. She lifted a stack of finished scripts and followed Lilly out the door.

Four

David Montgomery looked up and smiled warmly at his daughter-in-law as Jennifer was ushered into the elegant East side restaurant by a tuxedo-clad maître d'. Jennifer hurried forward to hug him.

"David, it's so good to see you . . ." She smiled at him and noticed the pronounced lines of fatigue and grief that edged his deepset eyes. The death of his only son had left its mark on David's gentle face and had aged him past his sixty-two years. He held her closely, then pulled back to look at her.

"You look great! Your job must be agreeing with you."

Jennifer was glad she'd decided to change from her usual working outfit of jeans and her precious silver baseball jacket to a new summer dress. She'd found it on sale at Saks Fifth Avenue, and had known instantly it was just the thing to wear to meet David for lunch. She knew that pink was a very flattering color for her, and this dress was perfect. The bright pink material was fashioned into a halter style, gathered at the waist into a softly flowing skirt. The bodice tied around her neck with bright pink silk ribbons. Matching ribbons encircled her waist, accentuating her slim figure.

"I bet you didn't know you would match the decor," David asked in mock seriousness. Startled, Jennifer looked around her and suddenly, they both laughed. The elegantly draped tablecloths and matching napkins were a soft pink color perfectly offsetting the color of Jennifer's dress. The restaurant, the dress, the new hairstyle, Jennifer smiled. She felt like a picture in a magazine herself.

"A toast to your new job," David said dramatically. The fragile glasses clinked together and Jennifer tasted the delicious cool white wine.

The hour passed too quickly as she told David everything about her new job. As the waiter served the escargot, dripping with butter and garlic, she related the events of her first few weeks, meeting Lilly, Ray and the excitement of watching a live television show in production. Over the veal cordon bleu, David listened attentively as she described an average day in the newsroom and the hectic pace she had come to love. Finally, as she finished her last spoonful of rich and delicious chocolate mousse, she told him about her escapades underneath Erica King's desk. David laughed and Jennifer realized how much she had missed talking to him. For months after Terry's death it had been too painful to see him, his physical resemblance to Terry and the depth of his own grief making it impossible. She realized now that it was important to keep in contact with this gentle, kind man. She smiled at him warmly.

"Thank you so much for lunch. I loved it."

"It was my pleasure," he answered smiling. He motioned for the check. "But I've got to get you back—I don't want Justin to be angry because I kept one of his star employees out too late for lunch."

Jennifer shifted uncomfortably. So far, she had been able to keep the conversation off the subject of Justin Bradley. She did not want to talk about him.

"Oh, I have a few minutes . . ." she replied casually. "Lilly said I could take a little bit longer lunch today, as it's a special occasion."

"Lilly's been a good friend to you, hasn't she?" David asked gently. Jennifer looked up at him and smiled.

"Yes," she nodded. "She's really great. She's taught me so much about my job and—" her voice wavered, "I've told her a lot about Terry . . ."

"Jennifer . . ." David's voice was suddenly serious. She looked up at him questioningly. "Do you have any *other* friends at I.B.S.?"

"Other friends?" she asked, confused. "Well . . . everyone is very nice, but I . . ."

"Jen . . ." David reached out and touched her slender hand. She looked into his concerned face. "There's something I want to talk to you about . . ." He hesitated as the waiter removed the dessert plates and moved away from the table.

"It's something that's very difficult to discuss," David said slowly. He took a deep breath. "When Terry died," he began. "A part of me died with him."

Jennifer felt a sob clutch her throat. She forced herself to concentrate on David's words.

"When Terry brought you to New York," he smiled at Jennifer, "I could see how much in love you were . . . I had never seen him happier. I knew how much he loved you, and—what was almost even more important to me—how much you loved him."

Jennifer fumbled with the napkin in her lap, trying to blink back the tears.

"At first, when Terry died," David said softly, "it was almost too much to bear, but . . . time heals . . . slowly. The days pass, and the weeks and the months and it doesn't hurt quite so much. You begin to understand that life goes on . . . there is a new day beginning every morning, and you have to go back to living your life . . ."

Jennifer looked up at him. She clutched his hand.

"I was very pleased when you started working," he told her, "because I knew that you'd be getting back into some kind of life—out of that tiny apartment and into the world again . . . but, there's been something I wanted to tell you." He looked at Jennifer closely. "Terry loved you very much, and the one thing he wanted most in this world was for you to be happy . . . It's no life for a beautiful young woman like you to live with a memory. You'll never forget Terry, and neither will I, but we can't stop living because we lose the people we love." He squeezed her hand gently. "I just want you to know that Terry loved you too much to want you to spend the rest of your life alone."

Jennifer felt the tears welling up inside her. She had been so confused, so many different feelings crowding her mind. Of course she would never forget Terry—their time together had been some of the happiest days of her life. But she was lonely, coming home from a long day at the news station with no one to talk to, no one to share the excitement of her new job. No, she realized . . . that was not what Terry would have wanted.

David smiled at her encouragingly and she smiled back at him, feeling a deep release of the anxiety in her heart. She had not admitted it to herself, but she realized now that these last two months and even today, dressing carefully with the hope of seeing a look of admiration in Justin Bradley's eyes, that deep in her heart she had been feeling guilty. She missed Terry, but already their time together seemed to be fading into a precious memory, a part of the past. David was right. She had to look to her future.

"By the way," David said casually as he reached for the check. "You haven't even mentioned Justin. How is it to work for him?"

At the mention of his name, Jennifer felt her face flush. Fortunately, the waiter arrived to retrieve the bill. She tried to collect her thoughts. Justin . . . what could she tell David about Justin?

"Well, what do you think?" David ripped his copy off the bill and handed the check to the hovering waiter.

"Oh well . . . Justin's very . . . um . . . interesting . . ." she finished lamely. David was looking at her strangely over his wine glass.

"You know," Jennifer said hurriedly, "I was wondering when Justin first came to International Broadcast Systems. Have you known him long?"

David's face relaxed into an easy smile.

"No, not too long. He's been at I.B.S. let's see . . . a little over two years. I met him when he joined the Racquet Club. He's got a terrific backhand."

Jennifer twirled her crystal wine glass, watching the pale golden liquid swirling inside it. She did not dare look up into David's face.

"Do you know where he worked before that?" She had wanted to ask Lilly what Justin had done before his move to New York City, but she had been afraid to ask too many questions.

"Well, let's see . . ." David settled back into his chair. "Well, I know he was a Vietnamese war correspondent right at the front lines and was awarded some kind of citation or award for the excellence of his work. When he got back to the United States, he was offered the job at International Broadcast Systems. At first he turned it down."

"Turned it down?" Jennifer asked incredulously. "Why?"

"I don't know." David sipped his wine thoughtfully. "I'm sure he knew he could handle the responsibility. I think," he seemed to consider his next words. "I think he didn't want to stay in one place . . . for some reason he seemed afraid of settling down in New York. As soon as his Vietnam stint was over, he seemed anxious to go back to Europe, to keep traveling. He finally agreed to take the position when he was assured he could continue to pursue his on-the-road journalism. He makes it a point of handling all the location work himself. That's why he has hired such an excellent staff at *Nightly News* to keep things going when he's away. And that's why . . ." David smiled at Jennifer affectionately, "It's such a compliment to you that he hired you for his news staff. It's one of the best in the country."

Jennifer nodded. The two sat and finished their wine in silence. Jennifer sighed softly, but David did not appear to hear her.

She had not spoken to Justin since the night he had kissed her. In fact, he seemed to make it a point of avoiding her whenever possible. And then, last week, it had been her turn to work the night shift again. Ray had gone down for dinner and she had been alone in the deserted offices. Looking up from her desk, she suddenly saw Justin, standing in the doorway of his office, staring at her. When she noticed him, he'd turned and walked away.

Lilly had asked her if Justin had mentioned her performance on the live show, but Jennifer found it impossible to confide in Lilly that, far from telling her she was doing a good job, Justin Bradley barely acknowledged her existence.

But then, yesterday, she'd heard laughter coming from Lilly's office. Walking over, she'd discovered Justin telling some funny anecdote about a past location shoot. Everyone was howling with laughter. As soon as she entered the group, Justin turned to her, a warm smile lighting his face.

"Jennifer," he'd said brightly, "I'm sorry you didn't hear that, but someone else will have to fill you in. I can only tell that story once a *year*."

She'd been so surprised by the tone of his voice that she barely had time to return his smile before he was moving away from her, striding down the long corridor to his office. She had stared after him, more confused by his sudden attempt at friendliness than she would have been if he hadn't spoken to her at all.

"Penny for your thoughts," David said, and Jennifer started. "With the way inflation's going," he continued, "maybe I should make that a quarter."

Both of them laughed, and Jennifer knew they did so not only because of David's quip, but out of relief that they'd finally began to rebuild their lives after Terry's death. Jennifer told David that she would see him again soon, that she would call him and let him know how she was doing, but she decided she would not tell him how she felt about Justin Bradley . . . not yet.

The offices of the *Nightly News* were buzzing with excitement when she returned. The long awaited location shoot in China was scheduled to begin the following day. Ray, Lilly, Justin and a full crew were to leave for two weeks in Peking. The rest of the staff would have to double up on their various responsibilities for the duration.

"Hi!" Lilly hurried by Jennifer's desk, her arms, as always, loaded with heavy scripts. "How was lunch?"

"Great—" Jennifer began, but Lilly interrupted her.

"That's terrific. Listen—you can tell me all about it later, okay? Right now, I really need your help. Everything about the China shoot has been changed about fifteen times today . . . I think Ray is having a nervous breakdown, and as for Justin . . . well . . . I'll believe I've gotten this crew safely to China when we get off the *plane*—" Jennifer followed her, trying to keep up with her rapid instructions. "Ray has moved the production meeting from two o'clock to one-thirty, so I'm already late . . . oh—" Lilly stopped suddenly. "Will you do me a favor?"

"Of course," Jennifer agreed hastily.

"Justin asked me to pick him up a sandwich when I went down to the deli for mine. Would you take the coffee and sandwich that's on the tray on my desk and bring it to him?"

Jennifer could feel the panic rising inside her. Go into Justin's office?

"Oh, Lilly . . ." she began, "couldn't you get someone else? I'm supposed to help Dennis with the running order and—"

"Jen!" Lilly snapped impatiently. "It will take five seconds! Give me a break!"

Jennifer looked at her harried friend.

"Hey," she reached out to touch Lilly's arm. "I'm sorry, of course I'll do it." She looked at Lilly closely. Her face was flushed, her eyes bright in her thin, pale face. "Lilly . . . are you feeling alright?"

"What?" Lilly finished stacking a pile of scripts and reached for her clipboard. She looked up at Jennifer's concerned face. "No, actually I feel lousy, but I figure it has something to do with the fact I haven't slept more than two hours a night since that famous morning I heard Justin say 'Let's do a location shoot in China!'" She attempted a smile, but Jennifer could see the strain in her face.

"I'll take Justin his lunch, and you tell me if there's anything else I can do."

She watched Lilly disappear down the corridor, running to make the production meeting already in progress.

Jennifer picked the flimsy cardboard tray up from Lilly's desk. She licked her lips nervously.

Jennifer's high heeled sandals made no noise as she walked across the soft beige carpet to Justin's office. His door was open. The chrome and leather chair was turned, facing the window. He was seated with his back to her talking on the phone.

Jennifer took a deep breath. If he didn't turn around, she could place the tray on the desk and leave unnoticed.

"Okay," Justin's clear voice filled the room. "I just want to make sure we've checked and double checked everything with the Chinese government. I want them to understand that I'll only film the usual places, the Great Wall, the Forbidden City, but I do want to film a lot of *people*, faces, children, young men, old men, and I want them to okay that too."

Jennifer slowly approached the glass desk. If she stood by the chair next to the desk and leaned over, she could place the tray close to him. She hesitated. The stacks of papers on the cluttered desk would make a precarious perch for the flimsy tray. Helplessly, she looked around the room for another place to put it.

Suddenly, Justin jumped to his feet and turned toward her. Frightened by the sudden movement, Jennifer fought to hold the tray which slipped in her hands. Justin froze. The phone in his hand was forgotten.

They stared at each other.

His icy blue eyes met hers, the thick heavy brows drawn down into a frown. Jennifer could hear the torrent of words escaping from the neglected phone. Moving slowly, Justin put the phone back to his ear.

"Tom," his voice sounded strained, "I'll call you back."

Jennifer had not moved. She forced her voice to sound casual and offhand. "I brought your lunch, Lilly asked me . . ."

Wordlessly, he reached to take the tray from her hands. His fingers touched hers and Jennifer felt the electric shock transmitted down her spine. Justin placed the tray carefully on a pile of books.

"Thank you," he said shortly. He did not pull his eyes away from her face.

"I . . . you're welcome." she stammered.

Justin reached across his desk and pulled a cigarette from a flat wooden case. The snap of his heavy gold cigarette lighter seemed unusually loud in the quiet office. He regarded her steadily through a light cloud of smoke. Jennifer forced herself to stand still. She didn't want to leave, not yet.

"Uh . . ." Justin cleared his throat, "Ray and Lilly tell me you're doing a very good job."

Jennifer smiled, relief washing over her at the friendly tone of his voice.

"I'm glad they're pleased," she told him, "Everyone's been very nice."

Justin inhaled deeply on his cigarette. He seemed to be searching for words.

"Have you . . . seen David lately?"

Jennifer tried to still the beating of her heart, tried not to imagine him circling the desk and touching her again.

"Yes," she answered. "He took me to lunch today. At the Sign of the Dove. It was wonderful."

Justin's eyes moved over her, taking in the dress, and the flowers entwined in her soft hair.

"He's a good man," he said shortly.

Jennifer nodded. Justin pushed idly through some papers on his desk. Suddenly, he raised his head and looked deeply into her eyes.

"I was very sorry," he said quietly, "about David's son being killed. I meant to tell you, but . . ." he raised his arm and let it fall in a gesture of futility, "it's been so busy around here, I just haven't . . ."

"I know . . . ." Jennifer answered softly, "it's all right . . ."

"So young," Justin said slowly, "such a crime . . . such an incredible *waste* . . . ." His voice was edged with a bitter anger.

"Yes . . ." Jennifer searched her mind for the words she wanted to say. "Yes" she repeated, "but today, at lunch, David told me that—that we have to go on living . . . when we lose someone we love," here she was forced to avert her eyes, "that we will always have our memories, but time will . . . ease the pain."

She looked up again to find Justin staring at her, his eyes suddenly dark in his handsome face. He placed his cigarette in an ashtray and started stacking scripts and schedules together quickly. Jennifer's mind raced. What had she said? David was right. No one should mourn forever.

"Now," Justin said, his voice crisp and businesslike. "I want you to take these down to Lilly and tell her they need to be revised as soon as possible." Reaching out, he handed Jennifer a heavy stack of paper. "And tell Ray to come in and see me before he confirms the travel arrangements."

Jennifer resisted an urge to bark back a quick "Yes *sir!*" She might as well give up trying to understand this man, she thought grimly—he was impossible!

"Do you have any questions?" he asked shortly.

Questions? Jennifer thought wryly. All kinds of questions. Like what, Mr. Justin Bradley, is your *problem?*

"No," she replied shortly, "no questions."

Turning quickly, she hurried out of the office.

"Jennifer?" Lilly's voice was breathless and she sounded very upset. The pre-dawn light bathed the apartment in shadows as Jennifer propped herself up on one elbow and looked at the digital clock on the night table. Six A.M. Alarmed, she sat up suddenly, clutching the phone.

"Lilly? What's wrong!"

"Oh, Jennifer, I hate to do this to you . . ." Lilly began, her voice hoarse and uneven. "I can't go." Her voice broke. Jennifer sat up in bed and tried to understand what Lilly was saying. She knew her friend was supposed to be leaving that morning with a film crew to shoot the China documentary. Jennifer had stayed with her in the office until eight o'clock the night before, making the final arrangements.

Jennifer listened as her friend began to cough into the phone.

"Jen . . . I can't believe it . . . all that work . . . and I . . . I've got the flu . . . I can't breathe and my head feels like it's going to fall off. Jen, can you go in my place?"

Go? To *China?*

"Lilly . . ." Jennifer could hear the panic in her own voice. "Lilly I *can't* . . . I've never done anything *like* that . . . I don't know what I'm supposed to do . . ."

"Oh, it's easy." Lilly interrupted her. "I've got it all set up . . . You just have to travel around with the crew, take edit notes and timings and keep track of the film reel numbers. The crew will help." She began to cough again. Jennifer waited, trying to will her mind to be awake and alert. She looked back at the clock. She had been asleep for only three hours. She had spent the sleepless night staring out her window. Thinking about Justin.

"Well, what do you say?" Lilly sounded on the verge of tears.

Jennifer tried again. "But, what about one of the others? They've all worked at I.B.S. longer than I have. Shouldn't one of them go?"

"They're all slated for other locations. Donald left yesterday, Karen and Mike aren't due back until the end of the week. And I know Justin won't want Tina to go—she hasn't had enough experience at the station."

Jennifer sat up quickly and pushed her hair back behind her ears. Justin. She had forgotten about Justin.

Justin would be directing the shoot. They would be together for two weeks in China. Suddenly, she remembered the sound of his voice when he had spoken to her in his office, remembered the cold indifference of his eyes upon her. Closing her eyes, she gripped the phone receiver tightly. She would be forced to work closely with him.

But would he even let go?

"Lilly . . . does Justin have any idea you're calling me?"

"No," Lilly answered hastily, "an old throwback to my freelance days . . . never call a producer and tell him at the last minute you can't do a job unless you have a replacement all lined up in the wings. Well, what do you say?"

China, The Great Wall, The Forbidden City . . . Justin.

"Okay. Lilly . . . you've got it."

"Great! I'll just call Justin and you can leave on the flight this morning. Is your passport up to date?"

Passport?

"Oh Lilly," Jennifer wailed. "I don't even *have* a passport!"

That was it then she thought, a nice idea while it lasted. But Jennifer underestimated Lilly. Years of dealing with the minute-to-minute crises that plague a newsroom had made her accustomed to solving unexpected problems.

"No passport . . . hmmm, now, let me think . . . the Press Department—that's it. They'll be able to get you a passport in a hurry. They send people all over the place at two minute's notice. Obviously, you won't be able to fly with the crew. You'll have to get a later flight. Let's see . . . the problem with that is there are so few flights. You may have to take the flight that goes to Paris, then to Pakistan."

Paris! Pakistan! Jennifer could not believe her ears. Maybe she was dreaming and she would wake up and hurry off to work and it would be a regular day.

"Okay, listen." Lilly's strained voice continued. "Call the press department and explain what happened. Talk to Charlie Coleman and he'll help you with your passport and travel arrangements. It's a long flight and you'll be on your own. The crew will have to fly ahead. Can you handle that?"

Alone. Jennifer felt a small fear clutch her heart. New York City to Peking, China by herself. Hours on airplanes, connections, strange cities.

"Jen?"

Jennifer took a deep breath. Of course she could handle it. No problem.

"Sure Lilly, I'll be fine."

"Okay, good luck—" A cough stopped Lilly's sentence. As Jennifer reached to hang up the phone, she heard Lilly's last words.

"I'll call Justin about the switch."

Jennifer hung up the phone slowly and leaned back to study the cracked ceiling. China. Justin. Working beside him all those days on location. Dreamily she remembered the warmth of his embrace, the touch of his lips on hers. The thought was almost too delicious, too comforting . . .

She sat up suddenly, a thought shattering her reverie. But what if he told Lilly he didn't want her to go? She swung her legs out of bed and stood up quickly. She would hurry to the office, see Charlie Coleman and get working on her passport. She wouldn't give Justin a chance to change the plans.

Jennifer showered and dressed quickly, one ear always tuned to hear the phone if it rang. By seven she was ready to leave for the office. Charlie would be in by eight-thirty. She could use the extra time to gather the papers and notes she would need from Lilly's well-ordered desk.

She reached for her keys and shoulderbag. Glancing back at the phone one more time, she allowed herself a small smile. The phone hadn't rung. Justin had said it was all right. She was on her way to China!

Five

"Excuse me, miss?"

Jennifer started. She was dancing across the wide expanse of China's Great Wall, Justin holding her in his arms as the pink dress swirled about them. He smiled into her eyes and then—

"Miss?" Someone touched her shoulder. Her eyes flew open.

"We've landed at Peking Airport."

The stewardess smiled at the confusion on Jennifer's face.

"I think you finally fell asleep about an hour ago . . ."

Peking Airport!

". . . If you come up front with me I'll get your knapsack out from the storage closet." The stewardess walked away down the narrow aisle.

Jennifer scrambled to her feet. Her neck felt stiff from her cramped sleeping position. Most of the other passengers had left the plane. Snapping open a pocket mirror, she hastily applied fresh lipstick and pulled a brush through her hair. Strange, she thought, peering into the mirror . . . I don't look tired, I don't feel tired, but I ought to. She was too confused to remember how many days had gone by. She knew it was eight A.M. only because that was the arrival time listed on her ticket. She had no idea what day it was. She had been awake practically throughout the entire trip. The last good sleep she could remember was the few hours before Lilly's phone call. How many days ago had that been?

"Here you go." The stewardess handed her the bulky knapsack. "Is someone meeting you?"

"Yes," she answered, smiling, "thank you."

Jennifer hurried down the passenger ramp into the terminal building. It was nearly empty. Lilly had mentioned that there were few flights per day into the airport. Jennifer went through customs and searched the terminal for a familiar face. There was none. Jennifer was left alone.

For the first time in the hours of traveling she felt her stomach twist with fear. What if no one came to meet her? What would she do? She looked about her and tried not to panic. Now only a few people milled about the clean, bright airport. Think, don't panic, she cautioned herself. What would Lilly do in a case like this? There must be an information booth some-where . . . someone who speaks English . . .

"Jennifer!"

She whirled around suddenly, almost dropping the knapsack. Coming quickly toward her across the cavernous space were Tony, Carl and Ray. They were running, waving.

"Hi!" Jennifer hurried toward them. It was strange to see their familiar faces in these unfamiliar surroundings. But, she noticed as she smiled at them, they looked the same as they always did. Even in China, they wore jeans and battered sweatshirts and run-down sneakers. The only difference was that each was clad in a silver baseball jacket like Jennifer's.

Ray reached out and pulled her to him in a friendly hug.

"Am I glad to see you guys!" She smiled up at him. "I realized when I couldn't find you, I didn't even know what hotel we're staying in, who our contact is here—nothing!"

"Wow!" Ray shook his head. "Lilly must have been really sick. That kind of information is basic! Of course," he looked down at Jennifer and frowned slightly, "*you* should have asked her."

Jennifer nodded. "You're right," she agreed, then added, "Do you think I'll *ever* learn everything about this business?" As she chatted, her eyes darted around. Where was Justin?

Ray's frown disappeared and he smiled at her warmly. "Are you kidding? You're doing fine. You should have seen Lilly on *her* first location shoot!"

The four walked out of the airport to the waiting cars. Jennifer thanked Lilly for one thing. She'd been right about the knapsack. The heavy bag, which Ray now carried out to the car, would be Jennifer's responsibility on the shoot. The crew would have their hands full.

"This way," Ray lead them out the exit doors. Jennifer licked her lips nervously. Now, she would see him. Justin would be waiting in the car. Maybe, he would even tell her he was glad to see her.

"Here we are!" Ray gestured to two shiny black cars in the airport parking lot. The drivers sat patiently behind the steering wheels. Another Chinese gentleman dressed in a dark gray business suit came forward to greet them. Despite her sense of excitement, Jennifer felt a slight sense of disappointment. There was no sign of Justin Bradley.

"Jennifer . . ." Ray said, touching her arm, "this is Mr. Liu, our interpreter and guide."

"Hello," Jennifer smiled at the gentle-eyed man.

"Welcome to Peking," he told her, shaking her hand formally. "I am here to help you, so if there is anything you need, please do not hesitate to ask."

"Something tells me," Ray laughed, "we'll need all the help we can get."

He then grabbed Jennifer's knapsack and threw it into the car's trunk.

"Tony, you and Carl divide the crew into the other cars, Jennifer and I will travel with Mr. Liu." His voice showed that he was anxious to get the first day's filming underway.

Jennifer struggled to hide her disappointment. She was determined not to ask Ray where Justin was. Ray watched her face for a moment in silence. He seemed to read her thoughts.

"Justin left this morning for the countryside," he told her offhandedly. "He took Dennis and a cameraman and went off to shoot outside the city. We don't expect him back for three or four days." Ray watched her face closely, but Jennifer was determined to show no reaction to his news. Turning her head, she stared out the window.

She considered Ray's information. Justin probably had a perfectly logical reason for leaving Peking the day she arrived. But, try as she might she could not ignore the nagging doubt which crept into her mind. She had spent hours on the airplane studying Lilly's carefully organized production notes. Justin had not been scheduled to leave the city until the following week. And one other detail stood out sharply in Jennifer's mind—the notes stated clearly that when Justin took his crew into the Chinese countryside Lilly—and now Jennifer—was assigned to go with him.

"I'm sorry you don't get any time to rest . . ." Ray's voice broke into her thoughts. "We all had a day to relax and get settled. I'm afraid we can't even stop by the hotel. You'll have to wait till tonight."

Jennifer turned to smile at his concerned face. He was such a thoughtful man, and had acted like a big brother ever since she joined the staff.

"I know. Lilly warned me. But it's fine really," she assured him. "I'll be all right."

The highway was only wide enough to accommodate two lanes of traffic, one traveling in each direction. Jennifer watched, fascinated, as two horse-drawn wooden carts rolled by piled high with cabbages. The two young men driving the carts were standing, leaning casually against the loosely piled vegetables. The stacks were as tall as they were. She was struck by the fact that both sides of the narrow highway lanes were crowded with bicycles.

"I'm surprised by the number of bicycles you have!" Jennifer told Mr. Liu, their official guide.

"Yes," he answered. "In the United States you have traffic jams because you have so many cars. In China we have traffic jams that are made up completely of bicycles. We have policemen on duty at five just to keep traffic flowing through the intersections, just like the American rush hour.

"The bicycle is also a means of transporting almost anything," Mr. Liu continued, "as you see there." He pointed out the window at an old man pedaling an ancient, wobbling bicycle. Strapped on the back of the bicycle was a large, squealing pig.

"Uphill, the man will get off and put a shoulder to the load to move it," Mr. Liu explained. "Downhill he will drive his bicycle in a zigzag pattern to avoid picking up to much speed and being unable to stop if necessary.

"Sounds like a real traffic hazard," Ray ventured.

"Yes," Mr. Liu agreed smiling slightly, "it is."

"There's our hotel," Ray interjected. He pointed to a building which faced the main street. "It's called the Min Zu." Ray pronounced the name carefully and Jennifer repeated it. She must have done it well, for her efforts earned a large smile from Mr. Liu.

The cabs slowed down as they encountered traffic in the city's main square. Jennifer turned to watch a number of old men performing some kind of ritualistic dance in the morning light. Mr. Liu followed her gaze.

"Those men are doing Tai Chi'," he told her. "I can best describe it as a combination of martial arts, meditation and . . ." he hesitated, "a form of ballet."

Jennifer watched, fascinated, as the men moved slowly and gracefully through a combination of stylized gestures. It was beautiful to watch.

"Wow . . ." Ray said softly as the cab driver leaned on his horn. "We're going to have real audio problems shooting around here. Is it always this noisy?"

Mr. Liu smiled. "The cities are so crowded," he explained. "I'm afraid there is a constant din."

"Well, *there*'s a reminder of home!" Jennifer laughed as a young man walked by their cab carrying a large stereo radio on his shoulder. The music blaring from it was deafening.

"Yes," Mr. Liu nodded. "In China everyone saves to buy himself first a bicycle, then a radio and finally a black and white television set."

Jennifer watched a group of men and women cross the street in front of them. A slight frown creased her forehead.

"Everyone seems to be wearing the same colors," she said slowly, "navy blue, or gray or green."

"Men and women in China," Mr. Liu told her, "have dressed alike and in those same basic colors for years."

Jennifer turned to him in surprise.

"Recently," he continued, "cloth in pastel shades has become available, but it is still very difficult to purchase. The women wait in line as soon as a shipment comes in. The cloth is sold out almost immediately."

"We're going to drive straight to the Great Wall and begin shooting as soon as we can get set up," Ray explained to her as the car began to leave the city and head back into the country. "Mr. Liu tells me it's a two-hour drive. Why don't you try and get some rest?"

"I'm not really tired," she answered brightly.

Ray shrugged in resignation. "Okay, have it your way, but if you're not going to sleep, let's get a little work done. I have two *hours* to teach you everything it's taken Lilly two *years* to learn."

Jennifer pulled her scripts and notes from her shoulderbag.

"We may have sometime at the end of next week for sightseeing," Ray continued. "But the work comes first."

She nodded emphatically. "Of course," she told him. "That's why we're here."

Ray smiled at her fondly, and turned his script to page one.

Ten hours later, Jennifer and Ray pulled themselves wearily up the front steps of the Min Zu hotel. The knapsack in Jennifer's hands felt as if it were filled with stones as she tried desperately not to drop it unceremoniously at the lobby desk. She almost succeeded.

Too tired to take in the details of the hotel lobby, she could only smile weakly when the friendly man behind the registration desk handed her the key to her room. Ray reached to pick up her knapsack and she didn't protest. The two walked silently to the waiting elevator. The small woman operating the elevator smiled at them. Ray greeted her with one of the Chinese phrases he knew.

"*Ni hao*," he said carefully. Hello.

Jennifer leaned against the back of the slow moving elevator and fought to keep her eyes open.

"Here we are." Ray led her off the elevator and down the deserted hallway. Her room was small but comfortable with two narrow beds, a bedside table and a desk. A balcony opened out onto the main thoroughfare.

"You did a great job," he said softly. "Now, rest up for tomorrow."

She turned to him and smiled, the exhaustion easing as she remembered what a wonderful day it had been. For the first time in many days, she stretched out luxuriously for a real sleep.

Ray had explained carefully what her duties would be and by the time the cars started up into the mountains to the Great Wall, she was confident she wouldn't disappoint him, or make any mistakes in front of Justin.

The ride up the steep incline had proven to be an unforgettable experience. Jennifer's heart pounded as their car climbed higher, then Jennifer suddenly grabbed Ray's arm excitedly.

"There it is!" she pointed. Ahead of them, twisting over the mountains in both directions was the spectacular structure she had only read about in history books.

"Wow!" Ray whistled softly in admiration. "Filming this is going to be a challenge."

Carl, Tony and Ray unpacked the equipment and began the complicated process of setting up to begin shooting. Jennifer stood beside Ray and, as the long day progessed, took detailed notes describing everything they filmed. By five o'clock Ray announced they were finished for the day. Carl pulled out his camera and snapped pictures of the crew waving from the top of the wall.

"Let's bring a souvenir back to Lilly," Jennifer suggested.

Carl stopped a passing tourist and asked him to take a picture of the entire crew. As the sun began to set, they stood arm in arm grinning at the camera. Jennifer knew it was a picture they would treasure for the rest of their lives. Yet again she couldn't help but feel a certain twinge of disappointment—if only Justin could be a part of these experiences.

"Do you feel like eating some dinner?" Ray's voice brought her back to her small room at the Min Zu hotel. Dinner—all she wanted to do was sleep forever. "We'll just eat in the hotel," Ray continued. "Everyone's exhausted."

She knew she should eat. They had all been so busy all day, she realized suddenly, they had never stopped for lunch.

"Okay." She attempted a smile. "I *am* hungry . . ."

"Good." Ray patted her shoulder encouragingly. "I'll be by to get you in half an hour."

Ray pulled himself up off the bed and headed for the door. He turned back to her. "Are you all right?" he asked gently.

Jennifer looked up at his concerned face. She nodded slowly.

"I'm fine." With an effort, she straightened her sagging shoulders. Frowning slightly, Ray turned and left the room.

Jennifer walked slowly to the small bathroom and turned the shower on full blast. She pulled off the rumpled clothes she had been living in for two days and let them fall in a heap on the floor. Sighing softly, she shut her eyes and felt the hot water cascading down her body. She lathered herself with a bar of the precious beauty soap she had bought in the Paris airport and shampooed her hair twice. She knew she had to hurry if she wanted to be on time for dinner, but the enticing massage of the hot water on her tired body was too delicious to rush.

Wrapping two skimpy towels around her hair and body, she stepped out of the shower and tiptoed back into her room. She stretched out on the narrow bed.

"Jennifer?" Her eyes flew to her watch. Eight o'clock! She'd fallen asleep.

"Jennifer?" The voice at the door repeated. She realized it was Ray. He knocked again. "Are you okay?" She sat up quickly clutching the thin towels around her. She couldn't open the door.

"Sure," she called to him. "I'll be right down."

"Okay." Ray sounded doubtful, but she heard his footsteps disappearing down the hall. As she jumped up from the bed and began to towel dry her hair she silently chastised herself—she didn't want to keep the guys waiting for their dinner. And there was another thing she realized as she brushed her hair. Despite Ray's helpfulness and concern, he was in charge of the crew. He was her boss and depended on her to fill Lilly's shoes. She wanted to prove to him that she could be right on time and ready to go just like everyone else. She wouldn't be late again.

Pulling a bright yellow T-shirt over her head, she tucked it into a clean pair of jeans, brushed mascara quickly onto her long black lashes. Grabbing her keys, she ran from the room.

Tony, Carl and Ray were standing in the lobby waiting for her, and she felt a little ashamed that not one of them showed impatience. They must be starving!

The food was delicious and they ordered plate after plate of hot, fragrant delicacies.

Finally, Jennifer folded her napkin and pushed back from the cluttered table.

Tony lit a cigarette and leaned back in his chair. He turned to Ray, and asked, "Where did Justin and the other guys go?"

Jennifer held a small cup of tea in her hands. At the mention of Justin's name she felt it slip slightly in her grasp. She put the fragile cup down gently.

"Justin?" Ray was finishing the last of the pressed duck. "He took Dennis and Mike, the other cameramen, into the countryside. He wanted to take pictures of the farmers in their fields, harvesting the crops, working with their families, you know . . . ."

"Yeah. . . ." Tony took a deep drag on his cigarette and watched as the smoke curled above his head. "But the thing I don't understand is, I read the schedule before we left New York and I thought we were all supposed to be shooting together on this first week and then in the second week Justin and Lilly," he turned to smile at Jennifer. "I mean Justin and *Jennifer*—were suposed to go out for the country shots. Why did Justin change everything around?"

Ray sipped his tea thoughtfully. It seemed to Jennifer that he had been wondering about the changes as well.

"To be honest," he answered slowly, "I have no idea. I stopped by his apartment to pick him up and heard him on the phone. I couldn't hear what he was saying, but I think it was Lilly explaining about the flu." Jennifer did not trust herself to look up. She felt her face flush. "Anyway, all the way to the airport he kept shuffling through all those pages that Lilly had put together for us. And then, halfway through the flight he told me he wanted the entire schedule changed."

"Did he tell you why?" Carl asked.

"No." Ray shook his head. "I asked him but he said he had his own reasons. I thought maybe it was Lilly's idea."

Jennifer looked up quickly and Ray smiled into her eyes.

"Maybe . . ." he reached out and touched her hand lightly, "maybe she thought you were nervous . . . so she suggested the change to give me a chance to show you the ropes before the acid test of working with Justin . . ."

Jennifer tried to smile back at him. Lilly's idea? She doubted it. She now knew, having been here in China a few days, that someone just couldn't hop on a train or a plane. Permission to travel from city to city had to be granted. Why had Justin gone to all the trouble of changing the schedule at the last minute? She looked down, twisting the cloth napkin in her lap. Justin had decided to leave for the countryside as soon as he discovered that she would be taking Lilly's place.

"Anyway, after Justin gets back," Ray continued, "the schedule will go on as planned. We'll finish filming and be back in Peking at the end of next week for the banquet."

The banquet. Jennifer forced herself to remember Lilly's careful instructions. Justin and the entire crew were to be hosts at a banquet given in honor of the Chinese government in gratitude for their gracious hospitality. Sometime in the next several days, she and Ray were to finalize the plans for the dinner. Vaguely, she wondered when they would possibly find the time.

"You know something else that has been bothering me," Carl turned to Ray. "Justin has been acting very strange lately." Ray and Tony nodded in agreement. "For the last few months," Carl continued, "he's been very unhappy and impatient with everybody. I don't know what's bothering him, but . . ." he hestitated, "ever since the night he got back from that location shoot in Europe he's been like a bear."

Jennifer stared at the porcelain cup in her hand. She remembered that night. She had relived it so many times in her mind. She remembered every detail, the soft sound of the elevator doors opening, the solid impact of Justin's body against hers . . . the passion of the seemingly endless kiss.

"And, on top of everything else," Jennifer tried to bring her attention back to Carl's voice, "the night before we left for China, Justin broke up with Erica."

Jennifer felt her heart skip a beat. She did not dare raise her eyes.

"Erica was really upset," Carl continued, "I guess she asked him what was wrong, why he didn't want to see her anymore, and he wouldn't tell her. He told her he *couldn't* tell her. She was really heartbroken. I think she was really in love with him." He turned to Jennifer and smiled, "One thing about a television news room—with all the hours you spend together, eventually you learn *everything* about everybody."

Jennifer shuddered and took a sip of the cool tea to steady herself. Two images kept recurring in her tired mind, the warmth of Justin's embrace, his holding her close and devouring her with his passionate kiss—and the icy chill of his blue eyes staring at her across the studio floor.

"Well, we're all set," Ray said cheerfully. He handed the check back to the waiter, and rose to leave. "We meet tomorrow in the hotel lobby at six A.M." Jennifer rose stifly and followed him out of the dining room. He looked closely at her pale face.

"Are you all right?" he asked her as Tony and Carl walked on ahead.

She turned back to look at him and smiled weakly. "I'm fine," she assured him—"just beat."

"I can understand that," Ray said emphatically. "You haven't had any sleep in days. Be sure and get some rest tonight."

They had ridden up in the elevator and he stopped in front of the door to her room. Suddenly, Jennifer wondered if she would be able to stay awake long enough to get undressed.

"Thank you," she said softly to Ray as they stood outside her door. "You helped me a lot today." He took her keys from her hand and unlocked the door. Gently, he touched her arm and guided her inside.

"It was my pleasure," he told her. He handed her back the keys. "Now get some sleep. We have a lot of work to do tomorrow."

For one brief moment Jennifer looked up at him smiling down at her and thought now nice it would be to hug him, to thank him for being so nice and understanding, to tell him what a good friend he had been. She looked up into his face. It was impossible.

He might think she meant it as more than a friendly hug. She didn't want to hurt him.

"Good night," she said simply. He turned to continue down the hall as she shut the door.

Six

Rain splashed across the roof of the Summer Palace of the Empress and dripped down on Tony, Ray, and Carl and Jennifer as they stood huddled under its ornate arches.

It was the morning of their fourth day of filming and they were right on schedule. They had followed Lilly's notes carefully and, with a full day of shooting here, they would have had their assignment completed by the time Justin and the rest of the crew returned from the country.

Jennifer pushed the damp hair back from her forehead. Tony stood next to her, cradling the camera in his arms, trying to keep it dry. Ray paced worriedly back and forth in the small space, his bright yellow slicker dripping with water. Carl and Tony looked at each other and shrugged.

"Ray," Carl began, "I think we have to face the fact that we can't work any more today. This rain is not going to let up."

Ray continued to pace nervously, holding his damp script at his side.

"We got most of what we were supposed to shoot," Jennifer offered hopefully. "We almost made it on time . . ."

"Almost! Almost!" Ray threw up a hand in exasperation. "I wanted to have everything done by the time they got back. I wanted to hand Justin the notes and say, 'Here it is, everything you asked us to film— the Great Wall, The Forbidden City, the Summer Palace . . .'"

"Well . . ." Carl winked at Jennifer, "two out of three isn't so bad . . ."

"What do you mean it isn't so bad?" Ray exploded. "It means we'll have to come back here and shoot again, it means I can't tell Justin that I delivered everything he asked me for."

Jennifer watched as Tony and Carl exchanged glances. They'd worked like slaves for four days, and tempers were getting short. It felt like weeks since she had seen her tiny apartment, or talked to Lilly, or ridden the crowded subway to work. And now, Justin was on his way back to the city. They would all be leaving for Shanghai in the morning.

"Come on, Ray" Tony was losing his patience. "You know as well as I do that there are extra days included in the schedule for just this reason. No one can predict the weather. Justin understands that."

He turned to Jennifer. "I guess I'm just disappointed it didn't all work out," he told her.

She felt sorry for him, knowing that he wanted to do a good job for Justin. The rain was dripping down his face and he looked tired and discouraged.

"I know you are," she said gently.

Ray had worked so hard in the last few days—they all had. As well as the famous landmarks, they had walked throughout the city trying to capture the feeling of daily life in China. They had worked together, helping each other, working for hours without a break, often forgetting to stop for lunch.

"Ray . . ." Jennifer said softly. "Tony is right. Justin will understand that we weren't able to get the last shots."

Ray nodded and tried to smile.

"You did a fine job," she told him, "and, besides the filming, we have the banquet organized as Lilly would have it. He'll be pleased."

"I'm sure he will," he agreed, "but it's just that, I don't know . . . I used to think I knew Justin very well. I've worked with him for over two years and he's taught me a lot about this business. But even though we've worked side by side for so long, we've never gotten to be, well . . ." he hesitated. "We've never gotten to be friends. Justin is never really close to anyone at I.B.S. Oh, he can play the part of a pal—one of the crew—but somehow he keeps himself apart from everyone, almost as if . . . as if he's afraid of getting *too* close . . . ." Ray seemed to have forgotten Jennifer was there as his thoughts rambled on. "I'm not really worried that he'll criticize the job I've done here. But . . . well, I used to be able to guess how he'd react, at least on a job. If he found fault with what we did, I could handle that. What's difficult for me is I don't know how he will react when he hears we are behind schedule, because I don't know how he'll react to *anything* anymore. Tony was right." He looked deeply into Jennifer's eyes, and she sensed that he was trying to make her understand. "Since that night Justin came back from the location shoot in Europe, he's been a different man. I want to ask him about it, I want to ask him if he's all right, but I can't bring myself to. I guess I know he won't answer me. He'll tell me everything is fine, and I know that won't be the truth." Jennifer watched the furrows crease Ray's forehead. She tried to stop the thoughts that crowded her mind, but she could not. Somehow she knew, in her heart, that she was linked to the mysterious changes in Justin Bradley—that something had happened when she'd walked into his sunlit office that had seemingly changed his life.

"Ray . . ." Tony sounded exasperated, "I can't stand holding this camera all day. What's your decision."

Ray looked down into Jennifer's eyes and smiled sadly. Shrugging his shoulders, he turned and led them running through the rain to the waiting cars.

The bedraggled crew, struggling with the bulky equipment, stumbled into the lobby of the Min Zu hotel. The hotel manager smiled as he watched them pull themselves wearily to where he stood behind the registration desk. They were not the first rain-soaked Americans he had seen that day.

Ray and Jennifer retrieved their room keys, and the manager turned and plucked a small piece of paper from the cubbyhole corresponding to Ray's room number. Ray read the brief message and turned to Jennifer with a rueful smile.

"Justin's back," he said simply. Jennifer almost dropped the heavy camera case. Ray continued, "He says everything went well in the country and he's assuming everything here is fine and we're all set to leave tomorrow," he sighed softly. "Shanghai here we come . . . I guess I'll go up and tell him where we stand on the shooting schedule. Will you make sure everyone is packed and ready to leave tomorrow morning at five A.M.?"

Jennifer nodded. Her knees felt as if they were about to give way beneath her. Justin was in the hotel.

"Here . . ." Ray reached to relieve her of the heavy case. "I'll take that."

"Are you going upstairs?" he asked.

"No," she looked over at the souvenir stand. "I want to buy some more postcards . . . you go ahead."

She walked slowly to the souvenir counter. Justin was back. Tomorrow she would see him. How would he react when he saw her? Had his decision to leave Peking for the countryside have anything to do with her arrival in the city?

Most important, how would she react?

Jennifer picked up two postcards and handed the small woman behind the counter a yuen, a thin paper bill. The woman handed her the change. Jennifer attempted to smile at the woman's concerned expression. Even though they did not speak the same language, it was clear to her that the woman saw she was upset and confused. She also knows I look like a mess! Jennifer thought wryly as she started toward the elevators. Whatever Justin's mood was, all she could do until then was wait—and worry. She would take a long hot shower, wash her hair, and try to sleep. She had never felt so tired in her life—and she was never so certain that sleep would elude her.

The faint morning light filtered through the curtains on the open window of the small hotel room. Five A.M. Jennifer pushed a strand of hair back from her sleepy face, and took one last look around the bare room, checking that she had packed everything into her knapsack. She knew she was stalling for time, waiting until the last minute to go down to the lobby. Glancing down at her watch, she gasped softly. It was time. Well, she thought as she tried to supress a nervous shudder, she couldn't avoid him forever.

"Good morning," Ray grinned as soon as he saw her.

Jennifer smiled back at him. "Do you ever get used to these hours?" she asked. "I tried to get to sleep early last night, but it was impossible."

Ray nodded sympathetically. "You never get used to them."

Jennifer stifled a yawn. She had sat up most of the night on her little balcony, watching the sleeping city, trying to believe she was really in China and that it was not all just a dream. She had finally fallen asleep a few hours before her alarm went off.

"Good morning."

Jennifer whirled at the sound of Justin's deep voice behind her, and had to stifle a gasp as she got her first look at him. He wore a beige safari jacket and a navy blue turtleneck sweater. His blue eyes were startling in his tanned face. For a moment, Justin stood looking at her closely, almost studying her. She looked back into his eyes, but could not read the expression they held.

"Everyone's here. We're ready to go," Ray told Justin. "Everything accounted for—people, baggage and equipment."

"Okay," Justin raised his voice as his eyes swept over Jennifer to the crowded lobby. "Jennifer and Ray will go with me and Mr. Liu. The rest of you share the other taxis. The plane for Shanghai leaves in an hour."

Jennifer tried to hide her look of relief—and feeling of delight—at Justin's words. Maybe he wasn't so opposed to her presence after all.

The shiny black cars pulled away from the Min Zu hotel. Justin lit a cigarette and settled back into the seat.

"Ray, let's go over the schedule again."

Jennifer pulled a note pad from her shoulderbag and wrote quickly as Justin outlined the shooting sequence. She found herself trying desperately to concentrate on his words, the names, places and dates she was scribbling, but she could not ignore the electric feeling of his body pressed against hers in the crowded car, the scent of his cologne, the rhythmic cadence of his voice.

The I.B.S. crew boarded a small plane for the one and a half hour flight to Shanghai. Carl came over and sat next to Jennifer.

"I suggest you take one of these," he said mischievously, handing her a Dramamine tablet. "Something tells me this is going to be a bumpy ride."

Jennifer had never been airsick in her life, but something in Carl's voice made her realize he probably knew what he was talking about. Later, as the small plane was buffeted by the wind, she was grateful she had taken his advice.

"You learn," Carl told her as the plane lurched suddenly, "to take a small medicine chest with you when you go on location."

Jennifer grinned at him. "Do you think I'll *ever* learn all this?"

Carl laughed shortly, "Are you kidding? For the first time at bat, you're doing great."

A fine rain was falling when they arrived at the Shanghai airport.

"Just what we need," Carl grumbled, as they piled out of the plane, "more rain."

"Mr. Bradley?" Justin stopped as a young Chinese man approached him. Smiling, Justin shook the man's hand.

"Mr. Chen, I'm—we're—glad to see you."

Jennifer knew from reading Lilly's notes that Mr. Chen would be accompanying the crew as they traveled throughout the villages. Now that they were all together, the job of interpreting for twelve Americans was too much for Mr. Liu to do alone.

Mr. Chen had cabs waiting to take everyone to the Peace Hotel. Jennifer sank wearily into the seat and, with a determined effort, fought the urge to close her eyes and rest. Mr. Chen leaned in the car door.

"May I join you?" he asked politely.

"Oh yes, please," Jennifer answered, sliding across the seat to make room for him.

"Mr. Bradley is going to join us," he told her.

"My name is Jennifer Montgomery," she told Mr. Chen hurriedly, trying to ignore the start of anticipation she felt. This part of the trip was becoming very interesting.

"I am glad to meet you, Jennifer," he replied, "but please, call me Peter. I am only a few years older than you, and 'Mr. Chen' makes me feel like an old man.

"Besides," he grinned, "when I studied in America, I got the impression you used first names all the time."

Jennifer smiled. She liked him instantly.

"All right, we're all set," Justin slid into the seat beside Peter and slammed the door. Jennifer felt her heart thump unevenly as she watched him smile warmly at their guide.

The cabs pulled out and moved slowly toward the center of Shanghai.

"I will take you directly to your hotel," Peter told them. "I have arranged for all of us to eat lunch at noon so you will have the afternoon free to begin shooting."

Justin nodded emphatically. "That will be just great. Thank you Mr. Chen."

"Please . . ." he answered catching Jennifer's eye and smiling as if at their own private joke, "call me Peter."

They piled out of the cars in front of the hotel. Ray moved through the disorderly array of people, camera equipment and luggage to where Jennifer struggled with her heavy knapsack.

"We have almost an hour before lunch," he told her. "Want to take a walk after you get unpacked?"

Jennifer looked up at his friendly, open face. Though she'd felt exhausted when they first landed, she didn't want to waste any precious spare time sleeping. After all, when in the world would she come back to China.

"Sure," she answered, straightening her shoulders. "Just give me fifteen minutes."

"Okay," he smiled at her. "I'll ask Mr. Chen if he'll go along with us."

"Call him Peter," she told him as they started up the stairs to the hotel, and she smiled mischievously. A few minutes later, as she hurried from her room down to the lobby, Ray and Peter were waiting for her.

"Mind if I come along?" Jennifer stifled a gasp as she heard a familiar voice close to her ear. Justin was leaning against the wall of the lobby, almost, Jennifer thought distractedly, as if he'd been waiting for her.

"Of course . . . I mean," she stammered, "of course you can join us. We're just going to take a little walk before lunch."

"Hi," Ray greeted Justin. His tone seemed short, and Jennifer thought for a moment she saw a look of disappointment cross Ray's face, but she couldn't be sure.

As the four of them moved slowly into the crowded streets of the city, Jennifer was struck again by the number of people in the streets and the parks. The stores were jammed with shoppers, just like New York City's huge department stores at Christmas time. It seemed impossible to comprehend that there were one billion people living China. Mr. Liu had told her that, although eighty percent of the population still lived on farms, the remaining twenty percent— as many people as lived in the entire United States— were left over to crowd the cities. And she remembered what Ray had told her: one out of every four human beings in the world was Chinese!

"Look!" Ray touched her arm and pointed to a movie marquee. A large picture of Katharine Hepburn and Spencer Tracy advertised *Guess Who's Coming to Dinner*, the movie currently showing.

"And look there," Ray read excitedly, *Singing in the Rain, Shane* and *The Black Stallion.*" Jennifer looked in delight at the familiar movie posters with the titles printed in large Chinese characters.

"Chinese people enjoy American movies," Peter told them, "because it gives them a chance to learn more about life in the United States."

"What is that?" Jennifer pointed to a large open air stall lined with shelves of books. In every vacant space on the ground people were sitting engrossed in reading the paperbacks and newspapers clutched in their hands.

"That is a street library," Peter answered. "They are very popular. For a penny you can rent a book or a newspaper and sit and read it."

"I'm surprised they can concentrate on reading in the midst of all these crowds," Ray marveled. "It's all I can do to keep my mind on a book in the quiet of my own home."

"Well actually," Peter explained, "the people you see here live in very small apartments, often with many members of their families. For them, being outside is a form of recreation in itself. Believe me, they would much rather be reading out here in the sunshine."

Jennifer walked alone beside Ray, trying to ignore her intense awareness of Justin's silent presence beside her. Once she felt his strong body brush her arm and she felt a delicious tingling sensation course through her. But she didn't dwell long on this reaction, her attention seized by a sight ahead.

"Look!" she said brightly, "a wedding!"

Ahead of them, standing stiffly to have their pictures taken, were a smiling bride and groom.

"What a lovely dress . . ." Jennifer breathed, admiring the white wedding gown.

"In China," Peter told her, "brides rent their wedding gowns, just as grooms rent their tuxedos. Everything goes back tomorrow, but it is a very efficient system."

Jennifer nodded, trying not to think about the expensive wedding gown stored in a box in her apartment in New York. Such a beautiful dress and she had only worn it for a few hours . . . .

"We seem to have attracted quite a crowd," Justin's deep voice broke into her thoughts. Looking behind them, Jennifer suddenly realized they were being followed by a large group of people.

Peter smiled, "A foreigner is never really alone in China," he told them. "The Chinese people are much too interested in you."

Jennifer and Ray exchanged a grin. All those days of filming in Peking had certainly taught them that!

"I do notice one thing that is very different in Chinese cities than in New York," Jennifer turned, as Justin continued thoughtfully, "there are no beggars in the streets. Here you have thousands and thousands of people living in a small space and yet the streets are clean and there is no one walking the streets in rags, asking for money."

"Yes," Peter agreed, nodding slowly, "that is true."

"I think . . ." Justin said, "that I know why. Would you mind if I tried out a theory on you?"

"Of course not," Peter smiled.

"Well . . ." Justin looked out over the milling throngs. "It seems to me that, despite everything—he wars, the destruction—your people have retained a deep self-respect, a feeling of pride in themselves and their home . . . and their home*land.*"

Peter nodded appreciatively. "I think you may be right," he said simply.

Jennifer looked up into Justin's thoughtful face, and was touched. She caught his eye, and the smile on her face was not returned.

"We should be getting back." His voice was suddenly brisk and businesslike again. Jennifer drew in her breath—he almost seemed to be trying to cover up the emotion he'd just shown. For one moment, she had glimpsed a side of Justin that she had never seen before; then the secret door had closed and he was remote and unreachable again. Had *anyone* ever been able to get close to him, she wondered, stopping to watch a family of smiling Chinese grouping themselves together for a snapshot. Had the invisible barrier that keeps everyone away from him ever been broken?

"Jennifer!" She looked up, startled at the urgency in Ray's voice. He waved and she ran to catch up, leaving her thoughts of Justin behind, as she hurried through the busy streets of Shanghai.

For what felt like the one-hundredth time, Jennifer pulled the crumpled production schedule from her shoulderbag and read the schedule for the next week of shooting. Justin did not want to spend much time in Shanghai, being anxious to take the crew to the more remote provinces where the Chinese people had never seen Americans before. From there, they would travel to the small town of Suzhou. Jennifer circled this location with a red pencil. Peter had told her that

Suzhou was called the "Venice of China" because of its many canals. Justin was interested in filming the beautiful gardens there, specifically, one called the Master of the Nets. Jennifer knew from reading Lilly's notes that part of the "Master of the Fisherman's Nets" garden had been reproduced at the Metropolitan Museum of Art. She had never gotten up to the museum to see the exhibit, she thought guiltily as she refolded the schedule, but never did she dream she'd be able to see the original!

"Excuse me . . ." Jennifer looked up to see a young Chinese man with an engaging smile standing next to her, "may I practice my English with you?"

Jennifer hesitated, looking over to where Ray and the crew were packing up the equipment. The long shooting day was over.

"Of course," she answered. Peter had told her that the Chinese people looked eagerly for any opportunity to practice their pronounciation. They learned English in school and from listening to the Voice of America broadcasts, but had little opportunity to actually converse in the language. A small crowd gathered around them as Jennifer and the young man spoke together. She found herself at a loss to explain some of the English figures of speech.

"What does it mean to say 'in spite of'?" the young man asked politely. Jennifer's mind raced. "Spite" meant anger or malice, but "in spite of" didn't have anything to do with anger, it meant . . . .

"Jennifer, we're leaving!" She turned to Carl and waved, relief washing over her. Saved by the bell!

"I'm sorry," she said quickly, "I have to leave now."

"Thank you very much," the young man said smiling.

Jennifer looked at his kind face, and decided to try a new word of her own.

"Dzai-jyan . . ." she said slowly, hoping she had pronounced it correctly. The young man smiled.

"Good-bye to you, too."

Jennifer blinked sleepily as she looked down at the postcard of Shanghai. She was trying to send Lilly one from every stop along the trip. It had been five minutes since she had carefully written "Dear Lilly" across the top of the card. There was so much she wanted to tell her friend, but somehow she couldn't find a way to begin. With her pen poised in mid-air, she found herself thinking back over the long day, the flight from Peking, the walk through Shanghai, the look on Justin's face when he talked with Peter about the spirit of the Chinese people. She knew she could find no fault in the way Justin was treating her. He had been courteous and polite. Then why did she feel this emptiness inside? Jennifer asked herself. Because, she admitted as she pushed Lilly's postcard away, you don't want him to treat you with courtesy. You want something more than that.

Stretching wearily, Jennifer moved to the narrow bed. Well, she thought, as she tried to sleep, at least he *is* talking to you. You should be grateful for that. But even as these thoughts passed through her mind another image haunted her, making sleep impossible. She closed her eyes, remembering his touch, the fire of his lips on hers, the crush of his embrace.

Then, when sleep had almost come, a dark fear seized her—would he never touch her again?

Seven

Jennifer clutched Ray's arm for support as the speeding van careened around another corner. The driver leaned on the horn, its blaring noise sending bicycles, children and farmers scattering in all directions.

"Do they always drive like this?" she whispered to Peter, who smiled at the frightened expression on her face.

"I'm afraid so," he answered. Jennifer shut her eyes as a large truck headed straight for the van. Miraculously, and with a blast of the horn, the driver swerved to miss the oncoming truck, then sped off down the road.

"You've got to admit," Ray said, attempting to smile, "they're awfully good at avoiding collisions."

Jennifer smiled thinly and tried to concentrate on the magnificent scenery flashing by the windows. The crew was headed to Chuangchou, a city in a remote province of the countryside. The van sped past acres of lush, green farmland. Mountains loomed on both sides of the road and Jennifer stared at the bright red pagodas perched on top of them. Workers toiled in the fields. Women with babies strapped to their backs stood swinging water-filled buckets. Water buffalos moved slowly past scarecrows decorated with fishing poles and brightly colored kerchiefs blowing in the wind.

"Everywhere you turn," Jennifer breathed, "it looks like a picture postcard."

Ray smiled at her. "I'm really impressed with the stone walls."

Jennifer followed his gaze to a long, low wall bordering a field. Stones of every shape and size were carefully placed together to form a structure that, while practical, was also a work of art.

"You see," Ray pointed, "in the middle of the wall the entire design changes, as if the mason got bored with one technique and decided to try something else."

"Oh look!" Jennifer pointed excitedly. On the side of the road a man had a small stand covered with round bamboo hats. "Peter," she cried pointing to the stand, "those are the hats I've been looking for. Do you think we could stop for a minute so I could buy one?"

Peter smiled at her. "Well," he shrugged. "We could use a moment to stretch our legs." Peter leaned forward and spoke to the driver and the van began to slow down.

Jennifer raced to the stand. The round hats were made of carefully woven bamboo. Forming a circle at the base, they came to a sharp point in the center. Jennifer placed one on top of her head. Two pieces of thin leather tied securely under her chin, keeping the hat in place.

"How much is it?" she asked Peter, who translated the man's reply. "Two yuen." Jennifer stared at him. The beautiful handmade hat cost one dollar. "I'll take two," she told him. She turned to Ray, laughing at the look on his face as he saw her in the hat. "Lilly will love one of these."

"Very fetching." She turned at the sound of Justin's disapproving voice. He frowned at Ray. "Were we scheduled to make a stop here?" Ray flushed and answered awkwardly, "No, but Jennifer saw these hats and Peter thought it might be a good idea if we stopped and stretched and . . ."

"Ray," Justin said his voice even and controlled, "Do I have to remind you that we are on a very tight schedule and if you really find it necessary to stop to buy Jennifer presents you might find a way to do it on your own time."

Jennifer gasped, as Justin turned and marched angrily back to the other van. Ray's face had gone white.

"Let's go," he said shortly, and strode back to the van.

"Ray," Jennifer rushed to catch up with him, feeling suddenly foolish in her bamboo hat. "Ray, it wasn't your fault we stopped. It was my idea. Justin shouldn't have gotten mad at you. If it was anybody's mistake it was mine."

"No . . ." Ray's mouth settled in a grim line. "Justin is absolutely right. It is up to me to keep us on schedule and, believe me," she saw him clench his fists tightly, "that is *exactly* what I am going to do . . ."

They rode on in silence, Jennifer trying to understand what had just happened. What had gotten into Justin anyway? They had only stopped for a minute, just to buy a souvenir for herself and Lilly. And what did he mean about Ray buying her presents? She had bought the hat for herself. She would have to find some time to explain what had happened to Justin. But at the thought of confronting him, she felt her breath catch in her throat.

"Don't you go and do anything stupid like telling Justin it was your fault," Ray said suddenly. She stared at him.

"The best thing to do," he continued, "is to go on with our jobs and just forget the whole thing, okay?"

She nodded. Forget the whole thing? She wondered if she could.

"I will say," Ray admitted grudgingly, as they unpacked the vans, "Justin was right about one thing. These people aren't used to seeing Americans." Jennifer looked up and nodded in agreement. The crew had arrived only ten minutes before, and already a crowd of almost sixty people surrounded the vans. Many seemed to be staring with particular interest at her.

Ray reached out and touched a strand of the long blonde hair which curled on her shoulder. "*That's* something definitely new to them," he told her, attempting to smile. "Peter told me that you are probably the first blonde these people have ever seen." Jennifer smiled back, relieved to see that he was be ginning to relax after his encounter with Justin. Ray turned back to the van. Jennifer reached for a box of cables and stopped. Justin was staring at her, his eyes dark and cold. She knew that he had seen Ray touching her hair.

"All set?" Ray asked cheerfully. She looked at him quickly. He had not seen Justin watching them.

"All set!" she answered quickly. Looking back, she saw Justin disappearing into the crowd.

Jennifer raised her face to feel the soothing warmth of the sun. She was standing next to Peter in one of the carefully planted fields that surrounded them in all directions. Tony and the other cameraman were setting up for the next shot and Carl had given everyone a five-minute break.

"I am resisting an urge," Jennifer told Peter, "to lie down right here in this field and fall asleep in the sun."

Peter smiled. "You have had a busy schedule," he agreed. He then turned as one of the farmers approached him with a question. Jennifer watched as the two engaged in a stilted conversation.

"Wow . . ." Peter shook his head when the man had moved away.

"What's wrong?" she asked him.

"The dialect here is very difficult to understand," he explained. "It is said that long ago the farmers tried to imitate the sounds of the birds. As a result their language has a very sing-song musical lilt to it that is rather unique."

Ray walked toward them across the field. Jennifer suddenly realized how tired he looked. The hectic schedule was taking its toll on everyone. She also knew that the heat and humidity were making it difficult for the crew to work long hours under the blazing sun.

"We should be able to quit in about two more hours," he told her, as if answering some unasked question. "I don't know about you, but that first beer, what was it—*pi-jiu*—is going to taste good."

Jennifer smiled at him in the heat. She wished she could wear her bamboo hat, but she knew the wisest thing to do was to leave those hats packed until she got back home.

"I'm really impressed," Ray was telling Peter, "by the way every square inch of farmland is used. They've planted right up to the roadside."

Peter nodded. "With so many people to feed, we cannot let even a tiny plot of land go untended. You will see farmers digging and planting on land where it is almost impossible to get a foothold. Vegetable gardens, even if there is only room for a few plants are everywhere. One of the main problems," he told them seriously, "is that, although there are 800 million people working on the farms, only ten percent of the land is suitable for crops."

Ray and Jennifer stared at him in amazement.

"Ray!" They turned quickly at the sound of Justin's voice. "Let's *go*!"

"Boy," Ray grumbled as he turned to walk back to the cameramen. "What is it with him—why doesn't he get off my *back*."

Jennifer followed him across the field wondering herself at the constantly changing moods of the man they worked for.

The Master of the Fisherman's Nets garden was even more beautiful than Jennifer had imagined. Graceful pagodas overlooked a small pond filled with bright orange goldfish. Flowers were everywhere, intermingled with uniquely sculptured trees. Mr. Liu explained that the architect had designed the garden so that every door and window in the pagodas framed a carefully balanced scene.

In the corner of the garden was a small pagoda with steps leading up to it. At the top of the steps was a small bench. Peter laughed as Jennifer ran up to sit inside the delicate structure.

"I feel like a princess inside this!" she called to Ray, who turned to her with an easy smile. Justin looked up at the sound of her voice, his dark eyebrows drawn together in a frown.

"Whoops . . . ." Jennifer muttered, hurrying down from her perch.

The crew spent the entire afternoon filming the exquisite garden, the bubbling spring, the small courtyards, Jennifer's favorite pagoda chair. She noticed the intense concentration that lit Justin's face as he moved slowly around the garden, softly telling Tony what shots to take.

"Take five!" Carl's voice was crisp and loud. A visible tension eased as the crew stopped to rest. Jennifer stretched wearily and looked for Peter. He was standing in the corner of the garden talking to a young man and woman. Their little girl clung to her mother's wide pants leg. Both the man and woman were wearing khaki green jackets and gray pants, but the little girl was dressed in a bright pink dress and wore a pink ribbon in her hair. Remembering what Mr. Liu had said about the scarcity of bright fabric, Jennifer was touched. What the woman must have gone through to get that dress.

Justin and Ray approached the group and Peter introduced them. Jennifer walked closer. The little girl was so beautiful. *Piao-liang*, that was the word Peter had taught her. *Piao-liang*—beautiful. Jennifer had a pocketful of "I Love New York" buttons to give away as gifts. She wondered if the little girl would take one.

Justin turned to Ray and began talking rapidly about the next shot. The little girl tilted her head, listening to the unfamiliar sound of the language. Suddenly, her baby voice pierced the air.

"Yang, yang, yang, yang, yang, yang!" she shouted.

Justin turned to her. Peter laughed, shaking his head in delight.

"She was imitating you!" he told Justin smiling. "That's the way your language sounds to her."

Justin looked down at the little girl partially hidden behind her mother. Throwing back his head, he laughed, a deep rich sound that caught everyone's attention. Kneeling, he brought his face even with the little girl's.

"Ni-hao," he said softly.

The little girl did not answer, but stared at him with wide dark eyes.

"Here . . ." Jennifer touched Justin's shoulder and handed him one of the shiny souvenir buttons. He looked up at her gratefully. Justin extended his hand. The little girl hesitated, then reached out a small fist for the button. She smiled shyly up at Justin.

"She is so lovely," Jennifer said to Peter. "Do you think she'll have many brothers and sisters?"

Peter looked at her, his voice suddenly quiet.

"No . . ." he said slowly, "she will be an only child."

Jennifer looked at him in confusion.

"Young couples in China are urged to have only one child," he explained. "China has such severe population problems, it is official policy to give a bonus to a couple who have only one child. The bonus must be returned if they have more."

Jennifer stared at the little girl, trying to understand the impact of Peter's words.

"In time," he continued, "there will be hundreds of millions of children, growing up in China as the sole object of their parents' love. There will be smaller families, fewer aunts and uncles . . ."

Jennifer looked at the young woman smiling down at her daughter. The little girl would be her only child.

"But . . ." her voice trailed off and Peter attempted to smile.

"If we do not control our population in some way," he told her simply, "there would soon not be room to walk."

"Okay, let's try it again!" Carl's voice prompted them all into immediate action. Moving back into her accustomed place, Jennifer watched Justin say good-bye to the little girl. Suddenly she wondered what kind of a father he would be, then stopped her thoughts instantly. Whatever was the matter with her, daydreaming like this?

"Action!" Carl yelled.

Jennifer turned to watch Justin move back to where Tony stood awaiting his instructions. The moment had passed, but she knew she would never forget it. Never forget the unfamiliar touch of gentleness in his dark eyes and the rich warm sound of his laughter.

"Good-bye, Peter," Jennifer said quietly trying hard to smile.

"Oh, come on," he said, grinning at her, "you can do better than that . . ."

"*Zai-jian,*" she said carefully and they both laughed.

"I'm sorry to go," she told him truthfully. "I'm very glad I got to know you."

Peter smiled at her. "I may come to New York someday soon. I studied in Los Angeles, and never got out there."

"Los Angeles?" Jennifer laughed. "So that accounts for your laid back attitude." He laughed at her remark, and shook her hand warmly.

"Good-bye, Peter. I mean, *zai-jian* . . ." Ray shook Peter's hand formally. Jennifer could hardly believe they had only met a week before. She felt that she had known Peter much longer.

"Have a wonderful trip back to Peking," he told her. "Who knows? Maybe you will be coming back to China again soon."

"Maybe . . ." she agreed, "but if we never see each other again, I want you to know you helped us more on this trip than you can imagine."

Peter walked away to say good-bye to Justin and the other members of the crew. Looking back, he stopped and waved.

"Zai-jian!" they called. He grinned and turned away. Ray and Jennifer watched him until he disappeared from view. Ray put his arm around Jennifer's shoulders.

"Hey, cheer up," he told her. "Tomorrow, we'll head back for a few more days in Peking and then home. That's not so bad is it? You look like it's the end of the world."

Jennifer looked up at him and attempted to smile. "I know," she agreed. "It's just that sometimes you meet someone like Peter and from the first moment you talk to him you know that there is something special about him, that you're going to be friends. I felt that way about him from the first day."

"I know what you mean . . ." Ray said softly looking down into her face. "I felt that way the first day I saw you."

Jennifer looked up at him suddenly, a feeling of panic gripping her heart. Oh no, she thought wildly. She had just about refused to let herself think about this possibility. She would never want to hurt Ray— nor become more than a friend.

"Are you guys coming? They have dinner ready for us in the hotel." Jennifer whirled at the sound of Carl's voice.

"Let's go." Ray smiled at her and she attempted to smile back. She would have to make him understand how she felt about him, but somehow she was not convinced she could.

Jennifer knew she could not sleep. The cool night air lifted the hair from her face as she stared out of the window of her hotel room. Suddenly, she knew where she wanted to be. She wanted to go back to the beautiful garden, to see it again in the moonlight.

Slipping out of her nightgown, she put on a pair of jeans and sneakers. Pulling a warm sweater over her head, she walked quietly into the deserted hallway. Feeling like a thief, she walked with as much assurance as possible out a side door of the hotel. She had no idea whether it was wise to be out walking through Suzhou alone, but something in the night breeze caused her to forget her fears. She had to get out of her hotel room, she had to be alone, and she wanted, more than anything, to see the garden again.

It may be closed she thought nervously as she approached its intricate gate, but, as she got nearer, she noticed that the gate was slightly open. She walked softly, her sneakers making no sound as she moved through the quiet night.

Her breath caught at the beauty of the scene in front of her. If possible, the garden was more lovely at night than it had been during the day. A full moon shone down on the goldfish pond touching the darting fish with a luminous light. The air was sweet and heavy with the scent of flowers.

Moving slowly, Jennifer circled the small pond. She stopped and looked up at the moon's full round face. A miracle, she thought, that this same moon which smiles down on me now, in China, is the same moon that shines down on my little apartment, so far away in New York. But what were the lyrics of that song Terry used to sing . . . "the moon belongs to everyone, the best things in life are free . . ."

She smiled inwardly, feeling the calm beauty of her surroundings giving peace to her heart. She realized that the pain of her loss had finally eased. She could remember Terry now, the songs he used to sing, the sound of his voice, the color of his eyes, and it no longer hurt. She could be grateful that she had known the love they had shared, but she knew now that David was right—time and love heals . . . Love. She watched a sudden ripple disturb the pond's calm surface. Could it be that she was finally ready to accept love again? . . .

A gentle breeze blew across her face and she shut her eyes. The image of one man alone crossed her mind. She remembered the sound of his voice, the music of his laughter. Today, as she'd seen Justin with that little girl, she'd imagined another little girl with his dark curly hair and deep blue eyes . . .

Stop it! she told herself angrily, shaking her head in confusion. On a mad impulse, she bent and picked up a small stone, flinging it into the quiet pond, disturbing its tranquility and sending the goldfish scrurrying in all directions. It was impossible. She felt a sharp surge of depression spoiling the beauty of the night. She meant nothing to Justin Bradley, and the sooner she realized it, the better off she would be.

With a determined sigh, she reached out to touch the soft petals of a flower. Such a peaceful place, cool and quiet and private. She breathed deeply.

Suddenly, her eyes focused on a tiny circle of light across the pond near the small pagoda bench. A firefly? She walked slowly forward, then froze. It wasn't a firefly—it was the glowing tip of a cigarette. She was not alone.

In a panic, she remembered that the gate had been open when she had walked into the garden. Someone was sitting inside the pagoda. She could see the dark shape in the moonlight. A man.

"I see someone else likes to take moonlight walks."

Jennifer felt a surge of terror suddenly displaced with a dual feeling of excitement and some apprehension.

It was Justin.

"Yes . . ." she answered softly. "You frightened me."

"I'm sorry . . ." his deep voice penetrated the still night. Looking up, she could see his rugged profile silhouetted against the fragile delicacy of the pagoda.

Jennifer couldn't breathe. The two seemed suspended in a timeless space.

"Come here . . ." he said gently, his voice rough with emotion. He reached out his hands to her. Without thinking, Jennifer moved forward and mounted the narrow steps. She felt Justin's hands warming her to the very depth of her soul.

"It's a beautiful spot, isn't it?" he breathed, looking down into her eyes. She strained to see his face in the dim light. She felt his nearness like a tangible force drawing her to him.

"Yes," she whispered.

He pulled her gently up the last step.

"It is beautiful here in the moonlight," his voice was soft and low. "And you . . ." he reached out to touch her hair, "are beautiful in the moonlight."

Jennifer held herself suspended, not thinking, not breathing.

"Piao-liang," he said softly. Beautiful.

His mouth descended on hers, chasing all her fears and doubts. Suddenly he was wrapping her up into the strong power of his arms, pulling her toward him, devouring her, taking her breath, robbing her of every feeling except his demanding mouth on hers.

After a long moment, he pulled away and murmured something against her ear.

"What?" she whispered eagerly. "I didn't hear . . ."

But he did not let her speak. His lips found her mouth again and his passion was only met by the fire in her heart. She pressed herself closer and closer to him, trying to melt into his very being, wanting to stand as one so she would never lose him.

Suddenly, a shudder passed through his massive frame and she felt rough hands grabbing her shoulders and pushing her away from him. Released suddenly from his embrace, she stumbled back, sitting sharply on the hard narrow bench. He turned away from her, his fists clenched in anger.

"Jennifer!" he shouted to the silent garden. "Jennifer!" She looked up at him in horror as she fought for breath, her heart pounding painfully.

"Jennifer!"

Her eyes widened. He was reciting her name as if to remind himself who she was!

With a strangled cry, she found herself on her feet, racing down the steps, circling the pond, her sneakers kicking the fine gravel, the tears streaming down her face. Her thoughts and emotions tumbled in a turmoil of confusion. She could feel nothing but a jagged pain as if her heart were being torn apart.

Blindly, she crashed through the garden gate and ran back to the hotel, finally reaching the sanctuary of her small room. Great racking sobs shook her body as she flung herself down on the bed, confusion and agony enveloping her mind. She had felt his arms around her and the passion of his kiss and had responded to his touch with a desire of her own. Why had he pushed her away, calling her name out into the night as though to remind himself that it was she, not someone else, standing in the circle of his arms.

She cried until there were no more tears and her ragged breath began to find an even rhythm again. Slowly, as the first shock subsided, anger began to take the place of heartache.

All right Mr. Justin Bradley she thought, suddenly throwing a pillow across the room. That's it. She'd stick it out while they were in China, but that was all. As soon as they got back home to New York, she'd quit.

But even as she made these rash plans for the future, she wondered if she would have the courage to carry them out. Could she walk away from the only man who had awakened feelings in her she thought had disappeared forever the night Terry died?

With a cry of anguish, Jennifer collapsed on the narrow bed. She knew the answer to all these questions. It was no.

Eight

Jennifer peered into the mirror in the bathroom, and tried to decide what to do with her hair. She had washed it carefully and it was flying around her head in the hot wind the blow dryer had provided. She couldn't wait to tell Lilly about the furor her blonde hair had created.

Impulsively, she decided not to sweep the shining hair up, but to let it hang loosely down her back. Taking the pink silk ribbon with the tiny flowers attached to it, she draped it over her head and tucked it behind her ears, tying it securely to let the ribbon and flowers cascade down her shoulder. She looked into the mirror and admired the effect. The ribbon kept the long hair away from her face, and the soft style suited her pink dress beautifully.

The last two days had been busy and tiring. The morning after she had seen Justin in the garden, the crew had returned to Shanghai and then traveled back to Peking. Jennifer had spent two days checking and re-checking the arrangements for the banquet. She could hardly believe that it was only one hour away.

Jennifer smoothed the silky fabric of the dress between her fingers and wondered how she would have felt if she had known, that spring afternoon when she had bought it in Saks Fifth Avenue, that she would wear it to a dinner for the Chinese government. The dress and sandals had survived their passage in the knapsack remarkably well. Jennifer twirled about the room, feeling the soft material brushing her legs, so cool and luxurious after so many days of wearing jeans.

"Jennifer?" She stopped suddenly, the room swirling and then righting itself.

"Jennifer?" It was Ray's voice.

"I'll be right there!" she called. She grabbed her keys and picked up the heavy shoulderbag. She stopped, staring at its bulging sides. Somehow, carrying it spoiled the effect of the flowing dress. Her eyes searched the room for an alternative and fell on her small green makeup case. She picked it up quickly and spilled its contents onto the bedside table. Taking her brush, lipstick and change purse, she slid them inside and snapped it shut. It looked like a fashionable clutch bag. She allowed herself a triumphant smile. American ingenuity!

Ray turned quickly as she opened the door. His long hair was combed neatly. He'd changed into a clean shirt and jeans and had attempted to secure a brightly colored tie around his neck. Jennifer couldn't help but smile at his freshly scrubbed face.

"Wow . . ." he breathed as he looked at Jennifer's dress and the soft, flowing hair. "The Chinese guys will never get over you."

She smiled back at him.

"You look good, too," she assured him.

Ray reached out a hand to her and she took it without thinking. It was warm and comforting. He looked down at their clasped hands and she followed his gaze. Caught up in the camaraderie of the moment, she made no attempt to remove it.

"Jen?" Ray turned to her, his warm brown eyes suddenly serious. Slowly, he dropped her hand and placed his arms around her slim waist.

"Jennifer, I," his voice began hesitantly. Jennifer could feel his warm arms around her and resisted. He was too nice—too nice to hurt.

"Ray . . ." she tried to keep her voice calm, "I—"

"I know you've been through a rough time . . ." Ray's voice continued without pause, "I mean . . . losing your husband and everything . . ."

Terry? Jennifer tried to concentrate on the image of Terry's face, but it seemed to be dim and blurry somehow. Ray's voice was gentle and soothing, "I've wanted to get close to you for a long time, but I knew you were just getting over what happened to him and I didn't want to rush you . . ."

Jennifer willed her mind to keep clear. She had to explain to Ray . . . yet, somehow, she couldn't speak. She felt herself being drawn into the sound of his voice, hypnotized by the warm pressure of his arms around her waist.

"I've been crazy about you since that first day." He was looking down into her eyes. She noticed, absently, that his dark brown eyes had tiny flecks of gold in them.

". . . but I knew you weren't ready for anyone else, that it was too soon . . ." he hesitated, then moved his hand up and gently touched her cheek. ". . . but here, in China, I've felt so close to you, working beside you. I've thought about nothing else . . . except . . ." He moved his finger down under her chin, ". . . except . . ." he repeated slowly, "that I wanted you."

Jennifer closed her eyes. She felt his soft lips touch hers in a gentle caress. His kiss was feathery light upon her mouth, fragile and delicate and achingly tender. She felt his arms tighten around her, trying to pull her close to him, but she could not yield her body to his embrace. Yet, dimly, she felt herself respond to him, this kind and sensitive man who had helped her so much. She reached up to touch his face . . .

"Well, I'm glad to see you enjoying yourselves!"

Soft as it was, the angry voice shattered the stillness. Jennifer and Ray whirled away from each other in confusion. They turned toward the voice and saw him, standing by the entrance to the elevator, his fists clenched, his dark eyes cold.

Justin.

Jennifer gasped and clutched Ray's arm for support. Justin's eyes bore into her, consuming her with their anger. She could hardly breathe.

He had never looked more handsome. He was dressed for the banquet in a navy three-piece suit that accentuated his broad shoulders, and a pale blue shirt brought out the color of his eyes.

The three stood staring at each other for a painful moment. Ray recovered first.

"Justin!" he said brightly. "Everything's all set for the banquet." Justin did not appear to hear him. He did not take his eyes off Jennifer's pale face.

"Yes," he said grimly, "you *do* seem to have everything under control here."

Jennifer felt the cold of his voice as an almost physical blow. She staggered. Ray held on to her.

"Hey, Justin . . ." Ray began, trying to smile. "We were just—" Justin held up a hand to stop him.

"Unless you people have forgotten," he directed every word at Jennifer, "we have a banquet to attend."

Turning on his heel, he strode back into the elevator and nodded curtly to the wide-eyed attendant. She pulled her hand from the doors, and they closed behind him.

The banquet given by International Broadcast Systems for their Chinese hosts was held at the embassy compound in Peking, a central modern building that housed the American embassy and several others. One of the large banquet halls had been set up with two large round tables to accommodate the *Nightly News* crew and their thirty guests.

Jennifer shifted uneasily in her seat and pushed her chopsticks idly at the food crowding her plate. A constant procession of waiters placed course after course in front of her, but she didn't feel hungry. She glanced over at Ray sitting across from her at the wide round table, but he did not notice her. She sighed and looked around the room. At least, she told herself, the banquet is going smoothly.

She and Ray had labored for hours over the menu, the seating plan, the guest list and the dozens of details involved in giving a banquet for forty people. She was pleased with the results of their efforts. Even Lilly couldn't have done it better.

Jennifer could see by the raised glasses that someone was about to propose another toast. It was Mr. Liu. Speaking in smooth English, and then translating into Chinese, Mr. Liu bade the *Nightly News* a farewell from China and wished Justin Bradley and his crew continued success in their project. Jennifer raised the small glass to her lips and dutifully drained its contents. The liquid seared her throat with a pleasant, warm sensation. She had long ago lost count of how many glasses of the potent liquor she'd had. Every time her glass was empty, a hurrying waiter immediately refilled it.

"I don't know how they handle this stuff," Carl leaned over to whisper in her ear.

She stared at the small glass in her hand. The Chinese called it Mao-Tai and she knew it was very potent, but she was too distracted to notice its effects. She felt numb, as if she were merely going through the motions, barely aware of what was happening around her. The scene at the elevator weighed too heavily on her mind.

She had not spoken to Ray since the encounter with Justin in the hotel hallway. She remembered how he had stood immobile beside her, his face pale and stricken.

"How *dare* he . . ." she closed her eyes thinking of the anger that had erupted in his voice.

"Here goes Justin," Carl's voice brought Jennifer back to the present. "This ought to be imteresting."

Jennifer looked up to see Justin moving slowly toward the microphone and quickly glanced across the table at Ray; he was staring at Justin, a muscle twitching in his cheek.

"I hope he gets this right," Carl said softly. She pulled her eyes from Ray's pale face and forced herself to watch Justin.

He approached the microphone and placed a small white notecard on the podium. Jennifer watched as he raised his dark head and smiled warmly at his guests. For some unknown reason she felt a surge of pride. His face was tan from days in the sun, and his dark hair shone under the overhead lights.

"He's been practicing for weeks!" Carl said excitedly.

Jennifer nodded. She knew what was about to happen. Justin was going to thank his hosts for their kindness and hospitality, and present them with a gift from all the staff at International Broadcast Systems. She could see the package which had been placed carefully beside the podium. She had wrapped it herself, agonizing with Ray over the paper and ribbon. The box held a beautiful Steuben glass apple. Lilly had carefully selected it as a symbol of the appreciation of the people of New York City, the "Big Apple," to the people of China.

Jennifer twisted her napkin nervously. It was not the nature of Justin's speech that had his staff breathlessly awaiting his words. He was going to give his speech in *Chinese*. They all knew he had practiced laboriously, but—

"Mr. Liu told us that in Chinese many words are the same, but their meaning changes by *how* you say them, how you make your voice rise and fall," Carl told her. "I have a feeling if Justin gets the inflection of these words wrong, he could end up giving a very different speech than the one he thinks he has written on that card."

Jennifer waited, her pulse racing. This speech was so important. They must not offend their Chinese hosts. She glanced quickly at Mr. Liu knowing that she would be able to judge by his reaction whether the speech was a success.

Justin raised his glass. All eyes turned to him expectantly.

"Ni-hao." Hello. Justin's deep voice filled the room. Jennifer watched as the Chinese guests smiled widely as they realized that Justin was addressing them in their own language. He did not falter, delivering the carefully rehearsed sentences perfectly. Mr. Liu's face relaxed into a proud grin. The room erupted in applause.

"He did it!" Carl reached out to clink his small glass against Jennifer's. They drained their glasses quickly. A waiter standing nearby hurried over to refill them.

Using Mr. Liu as interpreter for the remainder of his speech, Justin presented the glass apple to one of the government officials. He, in turn, toasted Justin and the people of New York. There was another toast. And another.

"I don't know how these people do it!" Carl marveled, holding his empty glass out to be refilled. "I have to be able to *work* tomorrow . . ."

Jennifer barely heard him. Justin had finished speaking and was making his way back to his seat. She felt herself staring at him, almost willing him to look at her. She could not pull her eyes from his face. He was shaking hands around the table, smiling and nodding. Eventually, he made it back to his empty seat. He pulled his chair back and sat down slowly. He raised his head and stared at her. Their eyes held for a painful moment. Feeling her face flush under his gaze, she dropped her eyes.

Jennifer struggled to control her turbulent emotions. She could feel a cold sweat breaking out on her forehead. Why did he have such an effect on her? she asked herself angrily. Why couldn't she even look at him without falling to pieces?

"I'll be right back," she whispered to Carl. She just had to get away from the crowd of people, have the chance to be alone for a minute to catch her breath.

Jennifer walked into the main lobby of the embassy. The air felt cooler here after the hot, stuffy banquet hall. She placed a cool hand against her burning cheek. Cold water. She would find the ladies' room and splash cold water on her face. As she moved across the lobby she noticed that her legs seemed strangely unsteady. The door of the ladies' room seemed to be moving farther and farther away with every step she took. After what seemed to be ages, she reached the door and pushed it firmly. It opened onto a floor-to-ceiling mirror. Jennifer stared at her blurred reflection. Her eyes seemed unnaturally bright, her cheeks flushed a deep red. Her hands felt shaky as she splashed cold water on her burning face. No more of those little glasses of liquor for her, she told herself. She pulled a brush slowly through her tangled hair. The banquet couldn't go on much longer, she knew. Soon she'd be able to go back to the hotel and sleep.

She stared into the gilt mirror and refreshed her lipstick. She knew she had to speak to Ray. She had to explain to him that it wasn't his fault Justin had been angry with them. She had to tell Ray the truth. She had to tell him that ever since the first day he saw her, Justin had not really wanted her on his news staff.

She threw the lipstick back into her purse and snapped it shut. Well, there was no reason for the situation to continue. She wasn't going to be the cause of any arguments between Justin and Ray. Ray loved his job and he and Justin had been, well, almost friends—until she came along. She squared her shoulders, feeling her body sway slightly. She would show him. She would show them all. As she'd resolved earlier, she would quit. She would walk into that sunny office with its stunning view and tell Justin that she didn't have to have it spelled out for her. If he didn't want her around, he didn't owe her any favors. Her image in the wide mirror seemed slightly distorted. She held her head up proudly. No, she had an even better idea. She wouldn't wait until they got back to New York—she'd walk in and tell Justin now.

She pushed the door open and walked back into the lobby. It seemed to be suddenly crowded wih people. She frowned in confusion. Had she been gone that long? It appeared that the banquet was over. She staggered slightly and held on to the arm of a nearby couch for support, then walked hesitantly toward the center of the room. Her eyes searched for Justin.

The crowd was thinning, the guests shaking hands with Justin and Mr. Liu and disappearing out the front door. Mr. Liu went back to find the rest of the crew, and Jennifer saw Justin standing alone, peering into the night through the open doors.

The floor seemed to be moving beneath her feet. With an effort, she tried to direct herself toward Justin. He seemed to be an indistinct blur. She tried to make her eyes focus. Suddenly he turned, and faced her squarely.

Justin.

Jennifer felt it again, the familiar feeling, from long ago, as if the lights were slowly dimming around her. The room began to turn slowly, like the merry-go-round in Central Park. The carpet seemed to be coming up to reach her. Her legs could not support her weight. She began to fall.

Strong arms held her up and cradled her like a broken doll. She struggled to open her eyes. Dark blue eyes stared into hers with a look she had never seen before mirrored in their depths.

"Justin?" From far away a shock wave seemed to touch her body as she heard her voice. She had never said his name before. The room kept spinning slowly. His name had such a lovely sound. She shut her eyes. "Justin . . ." Her voice seemed to be echoing down a long, empty corridor. She felt herself being lowered onto the soft carpet. The warm arms continued to hold her, keeping her safe. With an intense effort, she opened her eyes. The ruggedly handsome face was so close to hers. She reached up and touched his soft, dark hair. Vaguely, she remembered doing this before . . . but maybe it had only been a dream. She stared up into the warm blue eyes, so warm . . . yes— that was the difference. There was something in those eyes that she had only seen when she was asleep and dreaming.

Slowly, the arms tightened around her and she felt her body moving, as if floating through space. She wanted his mouth, wanted him to hold her forever, and yet somehow, the lights kept dimming. Her body was tingling cold and hot.

"Justin . . ." she whispered faintly. The light was fading slowly and completely. She shut her eyes and felt the darkness surround her, peaceful and quiet. A strangled sound suddenly pierced the silence, pulling her back from sinking into the night. Justin . . .

She felt strong arms tighten around her, lips press into her hair. Warm breath was against her ear, as she heard *his* deep rich voice whisper savagely.

"Monique . . . dear God . . . Monique *no* . . . please . . ." It was the last sound she heard before slipping off into blissful unconsciousness.

Nine

Jennifer opened her eyes and gazed dreamily at the clear white ceiling above her. She smiled to herself. Terry had finally done it. He had finally convinced the superintendent to fix the stained, cracked ceiling. Good job, she thought, a smile coming to her lips. They'd be so happy here.

Trying to lift her head she felt a sharp pain. She sank back against the pillow and looked around the room. She squinted her eyes and tried to identify the unfamiliar room in the gray dawn light. She finally realized it was not her tiny apartment on Bleeker Street in Greenwich Village. The images dimmed, then slowly became clearer. Suddenly she knew. She was lying in her room in the Min Zu Hotel in Peking, China. The thought came to her, the room swirled slightly in front of her eyes, and she fell asleep again.

Light was streaming through the windows of her balcony when she woke up hours later. It took her a few minutes to realize that she'd been awakened by a persistent knock on her door.

"Come in," she called weakly.

Ray, Tony and Carl filed quietly into her room. Tony was carrying a large box.

"How are you?" Ray asked her gently. He sat down beside her bed in a stiff-backed chair. He took her hand. "How are you feeling?" She felt the soft, dry touch of his skin against hers and looked up into his eyes. Images as indistinct as dreams swirled about inside her head. She tried to think clearly. He had held her hand before somewhere . . . She frowned, trying to remember . . . Oh yes . . . in the hall outside this room he had taken her hand in his and he had kissed her, and then something had happened to distort the picture, like sudden snow across a television screen . . . something had come to disrupt the harmony . . .

She clutched Ray's hand and tried to smile.

"I'm fine," she answered slowly. She couldn't remember what had happened.

"We brought you something," Tony handed her the large cardboard box. She got up on one elbow. Dimly, she realized she was wearing her long cotton nightgown.

The box was filled with soft tissue paper covering a pale blue robe. Flowers made from gold silken threads covered the brocade material. It tied around the waist with a wide gold sash.

"It's beautiful . . ." Jennifer said softly. She lowered her head to the pillow. It seemed like such an effort to sit up.

"You take it easy . . ." Carl said. "Doctor's orders."

Doctor? She turned to Ray. He was still holding her hand. The three sat in silence. Tony touched Carl's shoulder.

"We'll be down in the lobby," he told Ray, "and," he turned to Jennifer, "we'll be back to visit *you* later."

"Thank you for the robe." Jennifer felt tears of gratitude welling up inside her. So much had happened that she didn't understand. But she did know one thing—these men truly cared about her and the feeling warmed her heart.

Tony and Carl left the room, closing the door quietly behind them. Jennifer shut her eyes for a moment, trying to ease the dull ache in her head.

"Are you sure you're all right?" Ray's voice seemed strained and tired. She opened her eyes and looked at him closely. She tried to remember what had happened, tried to reconstruct the events of the night before, but so many pieces of the puzzle were missing. Ray seemed to watch the thoughts flicker across her face.

"What happened to me?" she asked him simply. He dropped her hand and moved from the bed to stare out of the balcony at the busy street.

She waited. Some of the pictures were coming back, the banquet, all that food and the clear glasses of liquor which burned her throat . . . the hot and airless room . . . the lights dimming slowly and a feeling that she couldn't breathe . . . .

"I'm not exactly sure," She pulled her mind back at the sound of Ray's voice. He turned back to the bed and, sitting down beside her again, picked up her hand. Absently, he twirled the thin gold wedding band on her ring finger.

"The doctor says you're suffering from exhaustion. You fainted in the lobby of the embassy compound. Do you remember that?"

Cold water splashing on a hot and burning face, thinking about something—what? Making a decision . . . searching for . . . Justin.

"Yes," she told Ray, trying to keep her voice calm and controlled. "I remember some of it . . ."

"Well, you were out cold. We came out of the banquet hall and you had collapsed on the floor. Justin was holding you."

Justin's arms, strong and warm, and his voice—what was it he had said? She'd heard him whisper, but couldn't remember. There was only a vague picture in her mind hazy and diffused like a pencil sketch that has been rubbed around the edges. He'd whispered her name—no, not hers, somebody else . . .

"They called the embassy doctor." Ray was not looking at her as he spoke, but staring down at the shiny ring moving beneath his fingers. Jennifer wondered if he even realized what he was doing. "He said your blood pressure was very low. You opened your eyes, but you didn't seem to know where you were, but then the doctor talked to you and you answered all his questions. Some color came back into your face, and he decided against taking you to the hospital . . ."

Jennifer frowned. She didn't remember the doctor at all.

"Anyway," Ray continued, "Mr. Liu brought the cars around and we bundled you up and brought you back here. The doctor kept asking us if we had seen you eating at the banquet and Carl told him you hadn't eaten anything . . . and then," Ray smiled suddenly at the memory, "he asked us how many toasts there had been. Carl figured at least ten. That seemed to explain a few things . . ."

Jennifer smiled with him. She remembered those small glasses. Ten, she knew, was a low estimate.

Some of the images came back to her tired mind, but she didn't want to remember anything more. She only wanted to close her eyes and sleep, but one important part of the story was missing.

"Ray . . ." she began tentatively, not really wanting to ask him the one question that was on her mind. His smile faded. He knew what she was going to ask. He dropped her hand.

"When the doctor first arrived, Justin was still holding you . . ." Ray stood up and began to pace up and down the narrow room. "The doctor tried to talk to him, but Justin wouldn't answer his questions. He wouldn't let you go."

Jennifer shut her eyes. Justin's arms holding her, his voice, whispering to her, saying something— what? If only she could remember . . . .

"We practically had to force him to lower you to the floor. I thought Tony was going to break his arm."

Something he had murmured so softly against her ear, his lips pressed into her hair . . . .

"I've never seen him like that," Ray shook his head. "He wouldn't talk to any of us. It was like we weren't even *there*. He just kept staring at your face and touching your hair . . ."

Those blue eyes—she had seen something there, something she had never seen before . . .

"He finally put you down. He lowered you very gently to the carpet. I was so busy with the doctor and worried about you, I really didn't notice what he did after that. A few hours later, after you were here, fast asleep, Mr. Liu told me he ran into Justin on the steps of the embassy. He said he'd never seen a man look like that before."

Jennifer looked closely into Ray's face. A cold fear touched her heart. She lifted herself up on one elbow with an intense effort.

"Ray," she said softly. "What did Mr. Liu tell you Justin looked like?"

Ray dropped his eyes then lifted them to stare directly into her face. His voice was cool and detached.

"Mr. Liu said that he looked . . . like a dead man."

She felt a wave of dizziness, and the room began to sway slightly like a boat on a turbulent sea. She fought for control, closing her eyes.

Justin, that deep, rich voice—she had to remember . . . Somehow she knew it was vital—had it been her name he'd whispered? No . . . she shook her head trying to clear it. No, he had said something else . . .

She opened her eyes. Ray was staring at her.

"I have to go," he said shortly, "the doctor said rest and quiet—" He turned to leave. "I should never have told you," he shook his head. "It doesn't make any sense." He looked back at her watching him. "But," he sighed softly, "I might as well tell you the rest of it—no one has seen Justin since last night. He never came back to the hotel."

Jennifer gasped softly. Instinctively, she moved to swing her legs out of the bed. They had to go and find him. Something was terribly wrong.

"Hey!" Ray moved quickly to the side of the bed and placed his hands on her shoulders. He looked down into her eyes. "There is no way you are getting up out of this bed," he told her sternly. "The doctor says maybe in two days or so, but not before. I don't know what's going on around here, what Justin's problems are, but I do know one thing—" she could see the determination in his clear brown eyes—"We were sent over here to film a documentary on China and that is what we're going to do. If Justin decided to take off, Tony and the rest of the crew will help me get this project completed. Which brings me to another point," he watched her face carefully. "I need you, too . . . I never should have made you work so hard those first few days without giving you a chance to get some sleep after all that traveling." She made a move to protest, but he silenced her with a wave of his hand. "I guess I was just too anxious to keep everything on schedule. I risked your health and the success of the entire trip and that was not necessary. You see," he smiled slightly, "you're never too old to learn. But the important thing to me now," he continued, "is that you get better and get back working with us and we get this film completed, so we can head on home."

Jennifer nodded. She was suddenly homesick for the dependable chaos of New York City. Ray bent over and kissed her lightly on the forehead. She put her legs back under the covers and settled back onto the pillows. Ray moved to the door. She saw him turn back as her eyes were closing.

"Jennifer . . ." She opened her eyes at the sound of his voice, "don't worry too much about Justin. Whatever his personal problems are, he's a professional. Forget what I said before about his just taking off—

my guess is he'll be waiting for us at the next location. This project means more to him than it does to any of us. He won't let us down."

Jennifer nodded weakly. She hoped he was right.

Ray smiled and walked out the door, closing it gently behind him, then heard his footsteps echoing down the hall.

Sleep . . . yes, she wanted to sleep. She had never felt so tired . . . But something was bothering her, something that made sleep impossible. An unanswered question kept repeating itself inside her weary mind. She closed her eyes. The touch of Justin's breath across her cheek, his voice so low and deep . . . She felt her eyelids become heavier and heavier, felt the dark edges of sleep surrounding her . . . She was beginning to remember . . . it had been a pretty and fragile name, spoken clear and soft . . . Moni . . . Moni . . .

Monique.

The darkness slid across her eyes, and she slept.

It was a familiar dream, one she had watched float across her mind so many times before. She watched it now, flowing through her memory like a warm, summer breeze. She could almost feel the world turning softly as they danced together . . . around and around to a gentle music. She was wearing a long pale blue robe with a wide gold sash and he was resplendent in a navy blue suit that brought out the color of his eyes.

They moved together, waltzing to the music, touched by the magic that held them as one. His arms were strong around her tiny waist, his hand warm in hers as they swirled around and around. The music faded softly, leaving them standing, breathless, in a cool and shadowed silence. And then she knew . . . knew in her very soul that now he would look down into her eyes, he would tighten his arm around her, he would cover her mouth with his and kiss her until they could kiss no longer.

She felt the warmth of his lips, the smooth touch of his cheek on hers. Such a beautiful dream, so warm and real . . . his arms around her, cradling her as if he had held her forever, gently in his arms so she would not fall . . .

Her eyes fluttered softly, but did not open. Such a delicious dream and a tender kiss so well remembered. She reached up to circle his neck with her arms, pulling him toward her, kissing him deeply, giving him back the warmth which seared her lips.

Her eyes flew open. She gasped against the warm mouth pressed against hers. It wasn't a dream! Justin pulled back and looked down into her bewildered eyes. He smiled slowly.

She reached up to touch his face. The skin was warm beneath her fingertips. Turning his head, he kissed her gently on her open palm, a touch as soft as a butterfly. Slowly, his arms tightened around her, pulling her up off the pillows, pressing her to him. His mouth came crashing down on hers and she felt herself being carried away on a tide of pleasure.

"Justin . . ." she murmured against his face, "Justin . . ." He did not let her speak. The only sound was the beating of her heart, the only feeling the strength of the arms that held her and demands of the mouth that possessed hers.

They were both shaking when Justin finally released her, placing her gently back against the pillows. Jennifer looked up at him, knowing her
feelings for him were reflected in her eyes. She made
no attempt to hide them.

Justin raised his hand and touched her face with a
long, thin finger, starting with her forehead and
slowly moving down to trace the outline of her cheek.
He brushed her eyelids and the tip of her nose, then
drew a line across her jaw and down the soft slope of
her neck.

She did not move. She was almost afraid to, afraid
to speak, afraid to shatter the stillness, fearing that
she would wake up and discover it was all a dream
after all. His eyes looked into hers with a glow she
had never seen mirrored in their depths.

Barely moving, he lowered his head to her lips and
kissed her again, lightly, tenderly, holding her head
cupped gently in his massive hands. He released her
slowly, caressing her shoulders and staring down
into her eyes. Vaguely, she remembered a time when
he had done this before, when she had felt his hands
on her shoulders and had seen his eyes blazing into
hers. So long ago she had felt the warmth of his
hands through the thin fabric of her dress, as now
she felt them burning through the fabric of her
nightgown.

They sat together on the narrow bed in silence,
sounds from outside wafting over them through the
open doors to the balcony.

"I've been such a fool . . ." Justin began, his voice
ragged with exhaustion, "such a fool . . ."

Jennifer lifted her hand to touch his mouth with her fingertips. He tried to speak against her hand but she silenced him with a gentle smile.

"You don't have to explain," she told him softly. "It doesn't matter . . ."

"But it does!" Justin exploded angrily. Suddenly, he was on his feet striding across the room to the balcony. Jennifer swung her legs over the side of the bed and stood up quickly. The room twisted at an insane angle, and then righted itself. She pulled the pale blue robe out of its box and wrapped it quickly around her, tightening the gold sash at her waist. She noticed for the first time how thin she'd become. She walked across the room to the open doors and stared at Justin, standing with his back to her, looking out on the streets of Peking. She waited for him to turn toward her.

Thoughts were racing through her confused mind. Justin's navy blue suit looked rumpled and she knew that he had not been back to the hotel all night. And yet, when he had returned, it seemed that he had come straight to her room. He had wanted to see her, to be with her, to hold her in his arms—to kiss her. What had happened between yesterday and today? Only then he had been furious with her. In fact, she remembered that last night at the banquet she had decided to quit on the spot, that she had finally understood that she could no longer work for a man who treated her so strangely, and she had gone to tell him so. From that moment, the memories were dim and distorted. But there was one thing that she did remember, something she somehow knew she must never mention to him unless he talked about it first.

When Justin had held her to keep her from falling to the embassy floor he had whispered a woman's name in her ear. Monique.

She waited. The cool breeze blew her hair about her face. Justin had not moved. She watched him, admiring the strength of his shoulders, wanted to cross the small balcony and press her face against his broad back and circle his waist with her arms. She wanted to force him to turn to her, to gather her up in his arms again.

She did not wait long. He turned to where she stood silhouetted in the doorway and reached out his arms to her. She almost flew across the small balcony, falling into his arms, then sighed deeply as he held her close, nuzzled against his chest. If she were still dreaming, she told herself, she hoped she never woke up!

She wanted always to be like this, to be near him, to feel him hold her against him. Eagerly she looked up into his eyes—and could not believe what she saw there. No longer full of love, they were expressionless. She drew in her breath, but before she had a chance to react, he lowered his head. His lips touched hers at first gently, then harshly as he drew her to him in a savage embrace. She felt a burning fire consuming her, searing to the core of her. And her mouth answered with passionate abandon.

"You should be back in bed," he whispered against her cheek, his voice husky with emotion. "That doctor will kill me." Gently, he lifted her, carried her across the room. He lowered her gently onto the bed. She held his hand against her burning cheek.

"Please don't go," she whispered. She couldn't let him go away. She couldn't let him leave her; she was so desperately afraid it *was* all a dream, and, if he ever walked away, he would never come back.

He leaned down. His lips felt cool on her burning flesh.

"I have to go," he told her simply, "I have a job to do."

She remembered then—the documentary . . . the shoot was almost over.

"The doctor says I need two days of rest, then I'll be up and around, she told him. Maybe, she thought wildly, maybe there was still time for them to dance together across the Great Wall of China . . . to swirl together in a magic dream across one of the seven wonders of the world . . .

"We'll see," he said softly. "You just get better first. You really scared me last night . . ."

She could see the concern on his face. He had been worried about her. Suddenly it dawned on her—when she had fainted in his arms, he had been frightened. But what in the world did that have to do with someone named Monique? Fighting her doubts, she smiled up at him, warm in the circle of his embrace.

"Yes" she told him playfully, "it was quite a dramatic entrance, crossing the lobby and collapsing in your arms . . ." she laughed lightly. "I remember now, I was going to tell you I was quitting."

She reached up to run her fingers through his shining hair. He pulled back slightly from her touch.

"What?" he asked shortly, a frown creasing his forehead. "What are you talking about?"

From far away, Jennifer saw a red light flash. A warning. She could see a frown replacing his gentle smile, a frown which threatened to turn his warm blue eyes distant again. She searched frantically for a way to turn back the clock, to make him forget her words. She wanted him only to remember the feel of his lips on hers. She wanted his mouth on hers . . .

She tried to make her voice light and casual, "Oh, you know—I guess I was just a little confused about ummmm . . ." She wished with all her heart she had never started this. She took a deep breath. She would say it quickly, and then she would reach up and pull his dark head down to her and make him kiss her again. "I guess I was just a little confused about your reaction to Ray . . . I mean what happened in the hall was really quite, well, harmless really . . ." Her voice wavered and stopped. She could see his face changing before her eyes.

"I forgot about Ray . . ." He got up from the bed quickly and walked away from her. She shut her eyes. His voice held the familiar icy tone she had come to dread. The dream was disintegrating, changing back to the nightmare she had lived with for so long.

"Justin . . ." she breathed softly, imploringly, but he did not hear her. She realized, numbly, he was already far away from her.

"Actually," his voice was cold and clipped, and she had to force herself to listen, "I had forgotten about Ray, but, more importantly, I had forgotten about *you* and Ray."

She was too tired. This couldn't be happening. It was an evil trick, for life to reach out and offer her paradise, and then snatch it from her grasp. She leaned back against the pillows. Maybe if she slept she could wake up again and he would be here, touching her eyelids, kissing her mouth.

Justin began to pace up and down the room. She summoned her courage and her strength.

"What about Ray and me," she asked him, a hint of anger in her voice.

Justin turned to stare at her. She noticed, for the first time, the dark circles of exhaustion underlining his deep blue eyes.

"I had just forgotten that you two were . . . what is the correct term . . . 'romantically involved'. . . ."

Jennifer gasped.

"But we're *not!*" she exclaimed. "He's my *friend!*" Justin's face transformed slowly, a malicious grin marring his handsome face. She tried to turn her face away, not wanting to see his familiar icy gaze, but it was impossible to escape the sound of his angry voice penetrating the silence.

"From where I was standing," he said slowly, each word falling between them like shattering glass, "that was pretty cozy behavior between friends."

Anger burst inside Jennifer's brain like exploding stars. Ray *was* her friend! He had been kind and understanding and *there* when she needed him, which was more than she could say for the man standing in front of her now. How *dare* he criticize her relationship with Ray.

"Okay," she said, feeling an icy chill envelop her body which had so recently been warmed by the fire his touch. "You think whatever you want to about Ray and me . . ."

Justin was not moving. He stood towering above her bed, his powerful body held in suspended fury.

"I don't have to justify my behavior to you or anyone else," she continued in a cold even tone. He moved away from her toward the window, and an icy cold reason came over her. Staring at him silhouetted by the light streaming through the window, she waited an instant, then aimed carefully, her eyes now burning into his.

"Who," she asked him quietly, "is Monique?"

Justin's face went white; he swayed slightly as if she had punched him. He stared at her in horror and, terrified, she knew that she had sent a dart stabbing into an old and festering wound. Desperately she wanted to take back the words, to tell him that she had never meant to hurt him.

"Justin—" She tried to get up, to stand on her feet to apologize. She stood up uncertainly, the room swirling around her. She just had to bring him back, to make everything right again. "Justin . . ." she forced the words through the tears which threatened to strangle her, then stumbled to where he stood immobile in the center of the room. She reached to touch him, but he recoiled from her hand.

"Justin . . ." she begged him. "Please—" He turned to her suddenly, his eyes blazing with hatred.

"Don't you ever . . . *ever* . . . mention her name!" He hissed at her between clenched teeth.

"I won't" she cried, the tears beginning to pour down her cheeks. She wanted to go back, to forget the last five minutes of her life. She wanted to feel him wrap his arms around her and never let her go.

He turned away from her and headed for the door.

"Justin!" she cried weakly, sinking onto the soft bed. She could feel the lights dimming. She struggled to hold on. "Justin, I'm sorry . . . please . . . ."

He did not stop. She closed her eyes, and heard the door slam.

"Justin . . ." she whispered into the empty room. "Justin . . ."

There was no answer, only a dark and unforgiving silence. She gathered the pillows into her arms and cried until the world went black, and there were no more tears.

Ten

As the 747 jumbo jet circled slowly and began it descent into New York's John F. Kennedy Interna tional Airport, Jennifer peered out of her window ex citedly. The lights of the city sparkled like diamond against the clear night sky.

Tony stretched contentedly and buckled his sea belt with a crisp click. He leaned next to her to watc the lights of New York come closer and closer.

"The Big Apple," he sighed, settling back for th plane's landing. "I am *really* glad to be back."

Jennifer turned to him and nodded. "I neve knew," she agreed with him, "how much I would mi it." She thought of the little apartment in Greenwic Village with its stained, cracked ceiling and its or window overlooking the city streets. She felt as if sh had been gone forever.

Ray and Carl were sitting together across the ais and Jennifer glanced quickly over at them. Ca smiled at her. Ray did not look up from the magazi on his lap.

"The captain has turned on the 'no smoking' sig and in a few minutes we will be beginning our a proach to New York's John F. Kennedy Airport," the stewardess announced.

Jennifer settled back in her seat. She would try to forget the unpleasant aspects of the trip right now, and relax. There would be more than enough time for worry later.

"Good night!" Jennifer called as she waved goodbye to Tony. They had shared a taxi from the airport and he had waited to make sure she got safely in the door of the quiet brownstone. She watched as the bright yellow cab disappeared down the street, and closed the door carefully. Glancing at her empty mailbox, she was glad she'd had time before leaving to ask the post office to hold her mail. The small box would have been overflowing. She would have to contact them tomorrow.

Tomorrow. The thought loomed as she wearily started up the narrow staircase—where would she ever get the strength to deal with tomorrow, going back to the office, to Lilly and . . .

"Jennifer? Is that you?"

Jennifer stopped with one foot on a creaking stair.

"Yes, Mrs. Maruzelli," she answered, trying to make her voice as cheery as possible, "It's me . . ."

The little old lady was peering at her from behind the safety chain locks of her apartment door.

"How are you, Mrs. Maruzelli?" Jennifer wondered if she could stay awake for this, or if she was going to end up asleep on the stairs.

"Okay, okay. . . ." Mrs. Maruzelli nodded. Jennifer knew by heart what the next question would be. Suddenly, she felt her shoulders sag dejectedly. It was all she could do to stand there.

"And how is that handsome man of yours?" Jennifer heard a sigh escape her. She turned to the lined face that she could barely see through the narrow opening of the door.

"Mrs. Maruzelli," she said slowly and clearly. "My husband is dead."

"Oh, my dear, I'm so sorry."

"I have to go up now," Jennifer said.

"I'll speak with you about it soon—I promise."

The old woman nodded, and softly closed her door. Jennifer continued up the stairs, but somehow she didn't feel as tired as she had before. In astonishment she realized that she felt relieved, as if some kind of weight had been taken from her shoulders. A sudden realization came to her—had she kept the truth from Mrs. Maruzelli not to protect the elderly woman—but to keep her own dreams of Terry alive?

When Jennifer's alarm woke her the next morning she had one thought on her mind. She had not seen Justin Bradley since he had stormed out of her hotel room, staying in bed for two days, waking on the third eager to get back to work. Tony had met her in the hotel lobby, his usually friendly and relaxed face looking drawn and tense. He explained to her that Justin, Ray, Carl and the rest of the crew had been working non-stop for the two days she'd been ill. Tony described Justin as a "man possessed," pushing them all to the limit, working late into the night. Neither Tony nor Carl had been able to understand the sudden tension and thinly veiled hostility between Justin and Ray.

Jennifer could remember Tony's words clearly. "After two days of working almost around the clock," he'd told her, "Justin announced that he was leaving for New York. He told Ray that the rest of us could finish, but that the most important part of the documentary was completed, and he had to get back to New York immediately." Jennifer had stared at Tony in disbelief, the impact of his words slowly becoming clear in her mind.

Justin . . . Justin had known she would be up and around in two days. He had made sure he would be leaving China as soon as she was ready to go back to work. He was not going to see her again.

Jennifer pulled herself up off the crumpled brass bed and put on a pot of coffee. She had to think. What was she going to do about this situation—Justin, her job, her entire life, for heaven's sake? In the midst of all the confusion and illness, the tears and the sadness, she had been certain of only one true feeling—she had loved Justin from the first time he kissed her, from the first time she had felt his arms around her. And she knew, more than she had ever known anything in her life, that she had not imagined the look in his eyes when he had held her close to him in a small hotel thousands of miles away. She knew, in her heart, that he loved her, too.

Jennifer could smell the coffee brewing, and went to pour herself a cup. As she drank it she looked around the small apartment and remembered last night's encounter with Mrs. Maruzelli, and the strength that finally telling the truth had given her.

She would need all that strength to face Justin, and to tell him that she was ready to love . . . again.

"Okay, okay, that's *it*! I've *had* it!" Lilly burst into Jennifer's tiny office and slammed her clipboard down on the desk. Jennifer looked up at her friend's angry face, but Lilly did not give her a chance to speak. "I'm telling you Jen . . ." Lilly collapsed into the only other chair in the crowded office. "I'm telling you I've come to the end of my rope." Jennifer waited for her next words, but she already knew what Lilly was going to say.

"I don't know what happened to you people over there in China," she began, the short curls surrounding her face bobbing wildly as she shook her head in frustration. "I don't know what happened, but I do know one thing. Ever since Justin and the crew got back, nothing has been the same around here. It's driving me *crazy* . . ." She stood up suddenly and began to pace back and forth, ticking off items on her long thin fingers. "First, you and Ray are barely speaking to each other. I don't know, it was none of my business, but I thought you kind of made a nice couple. He was really thrilled when I called to tell him you'd be going along to China and I figured the two of you would have a great time. Now, you come back and you're acting like complete strangers. Second, Justin isn't speaking to *anybody*. I asked him yesterday about Ray's promotion and he just stared at me, like it was the last thing on his mind. That puts me in a great position. I can't do anything about *my* promotion until Ray's is put through. Third . . ." She stopped her frantic pacing and turned to look squarely at Jennifer's face. "And third—you came in here like gangbusters that first day back, but now you look as pale and thin as you did that first day I saw you standing in Justin's office."

Lilly sat back down into the chair and leaned over the desk, her voice quiet and intense. "What is it? What *happened* over there?"

Jennifer made no move to answer. How could she tell her that she'd arrived home finally ready to leave the past behind her where it belonged, finally ready to tell Justin she loved him—when he'd avoided all contact with her. She wanted desperately to talk to him, but he wouldn't let her. He acted as if she didn't exist.

One day she had literally collided with him at the water cooler. For a wild moment, she thought that finally he'd have to listen to her. But her words had died in her throat when he moved stiffly away from her. The look in his eyes as he moved away from her, had left her trembling.

"Jen . . . ?" Lilly reached out and touched her on the shoulder, but she barely felt it. She knew what she had to do. Despite her new-found strength, she'd hung back, waiting for a cue from Justin. When that hadn't come, she'd let an intolerable situation, one that affected the entire staff, continue.

"Well . . ." She tried to think of how to answer Lilly's questions, "You're right about something important happening to all of us when we went over to China." Lilly was listening carefully to every word. Jennifer took a deep breath. "Something *did* happen to change everything . . . but . . ." she stood up sud-

denly, shuffling the papers on her desk into a neat
stack. She looked down at Lilly and smiled. Her
strength had returned.

"But," she repeated, "I know what to do to make
things right again, something I should have done the
first day we got back."

Lilly was frowning. "What are you going to do?" she
asked nervously.

Jennifer took her brush from her shoulderbag and
pulled it through her hair. She freshened her lipstick
and sprayed perfume behind her ears. Lilly looked up
and watched her in amazement.

"Jen," Lilly began, "are you going to tell me what
you're up to?"

She would go into Justin's office. She would wait
till he completed one of his endless phone calls and
she would tell him she had to speak to him. She
would find a way to make him listen to her.

"I've got to talk to Justin," she told Lilly simply. "I'll
see you later."

She left Lilly staring at her in confusion and
started down the long corridor. She knew what she
had to do. She had to confront him, this man she
loved. Somehow make him know what was in her
heart. And she knew what a risk that was. After he
had heard what she had to say, Justin would either
reach out to her, fold her in his arms and hold her
close—or he would turn away from her, and she
would be out of his life forever.

Justin's office was empty. Through the huge window, Jennifer noticed absently that the view of the
city already had the look of fall about it. The leaves

were beginning to turn. It was the start of another season. Jennifer crossed the room and eased herself down into the chair that faced the desk. It did not seem possible that it had only been five months since she had first entered this room, had first met Justin Bradley.

Where was he? Probably at a meeting. She considered going back to her desk and asking his assistant to let her know when he was back, but decided against it. If she walked out of his office now, she would never find the courage to come back.

She tried not to think about the first time she had seen Justin, but her mind kept going back to that spring day when she had first watched him walking back and forth in front of his huge desk. She would never forget the look on his face when he had seen her sitting across from him. . . .

Jennifer moved restlessly in the uncomfortable chair, and began to twist her wedding ring around and around her finger. She tried to concentrate on what she would say when he walked through the door. And no matter how he felt about her she had to convince him that Ray and Lilly should get their promotions. She turned the ring faster and faster. She would offer to leave International Broadcast Systems if he asked her to.

But there was one thing she would do before she left his office. She would make him understand how much she loved him . . . .

Suddenly the ring flew off her hand, falling to the floor and disappearing into the long shag carpet under the desk.

"Oh, no . . ." she groaned.

Moving quickly, she got down on her hands and knees and began combing her fingers through the heavy shag rug, searching for the thin gold band. She crawled farther and farther under the desk, sweeping her arms out beside her in wide circles. It has to be here, she thought frantically. Suddenly, she saw it, gleaming in the sunlight that shone through the window. Resting on her heels, she picked up the ring and slipped it back on her finger. She looked up and realized she was sitting underneath the center of Justin's huge glass desk. She moved to crawl back out, but stopped suddenly. Something on the surface of the desk above her caught her eye. A picture had been turned over on the desk top, its image directed down toward the floor. It was a picture of some-one . . . a woman. Jennifer raised herself slightly, trying to see it more clearly. Something about it looked strangely familiar. She turned her head slightly to bring the woman's face into focus.

She gasped and clamped a hand quickly over her mouth to stifle a scream. She was staring up into her own eyes, looking into a reflection of her own face, almost as if she was looking into a mirror. The picture turned face-down on Justin Bradley's desk was a picture of her!

Quickly pulling herself out from under the desk she began to push the stacks of papers and books aside. Her heart pounded painfully. She had to be wrong. It had to be someone else.

She found the picture at the bottom of a heavy pile of scripts. It was impossible to know how long it had been there. She lifted it up and stared: her own brown eyes gazed back at her calmly.

She walked slowly around the desk to the light of the window. Her hands were shaking as she studied the picture closely. She frowned. Something about it seemed very strange, something she couldn't quite identify.

It was a black and white picture, a standard eight by ten glossy print. Jennifer's face was framed tightly in a close-up shot. She had never seen the picture before. Where had it been taken?

The background looked European, like a cover she had seen on a travel brochure. Mountains and a small church were visible behind her head. Jennifer felt a cold chill touch her heart. Until her trip to China, she had never been out of the United States, but somehow she knew this picture had not been taken in America.

And there was something else. In the picture she was wearing a white coat with a collar of soft, fluffy fur surrounding her face. Jennifer knew she had never worn a coat like that.

She tried to still the panic rising inside her. Questions kept tumbling over each other in her mind. Where would Justin get a picture of her? From David? And, it if *was* a picture of her, why had Justin had the background changed to represent a place she had never been?

She searched the face for a clue, some answer to the mystery. The large eyes with the long, black lashes, the honey blond hair were the same she had seen every day of her life. In the picture, her hair was pulled back away from her face by two ornate combs. Terry had given her the only pair of combs she had ever had, and they had been decorated with hand-

painted flowers. She looked carefully. The two combs
which held the hair back from the smiling face in the
picture were carved in the shape of two small birds.
Jennifer knew she had never owned anything like
them.

It couldn't be her, she told herself, it's impossible . . . But then she was struck by another question
that sent her mind reeling in terror. If it wasn't a picture of her, who *was* it?

She heard a faint sound, and turned—Justin was
staring at her from the doorway. He moved slowly
into his office and quietly shut the door behind him.

Looking into her eyes he said evenly, "So, now you
know . . ."

Jennifer stared at him. Her voice seemed to be
coming from far away.

"Know?" she whispered, "know what?"

Justin smiled thinly. "You mean," he asked her,
"you haven't been able to figure it out?"

"Justin . . ." Jennifer fought to keep calm, "Justin . . . who *is* this woman?"

Justin looked at her sadly. She saw pain and sorrow in his intense dark eyes, the same anguish she
had seen reflected in his face on that first day they
met.

"Justin," she repeated. "Is this a picture of me?"

He looked into her eyes and shook his head slowly.

"No . . ." he said softly. "It isn't you. Maybe I
wanted it to be, but it isn't. No, it's not a picture of
you . . . it is—it was—my wife."

Jennifer reached out to the heavy desk for support
and stared down at the picture in her hand.

Lilly had told her that Justin had never been married. She'd said that he was one of New York's most eligible bachelors, rich, handsome . . . but now, she was holding a picture of his wife, a woman who had her own face.

Justin moved to the desk and sat down heavily in the chair. He leaned forward and put his elbows on the desk, then covered his face with his hands.

"But . . ." Jennifer's words were faint, "I don't understand . . ." He motioned her into the chrome and leather chair behind the desk. They sat in silence.

"That first day I saw you," Justin began softly, "I couldn't believe my eyes . . . I looked up and saw you sitting in this chair in front of my desk and thought I had been granted a pardon, been offered an escape from this endless nightmare, given another chance." Jennifer leaned forward trying to hear what he was saying. His deep voice continued. "I kept staring at your face, thinking how beautiful you were and how you really hadn't changed since the last time . . ." his voice broke. He started again, staring out the window behind Jennifer's head.

"But then," he hesitated, "then you started talking to me. I heard your voice and I began to understand . . . It wasn't true—I hadn't been given a second chance." He pulled his eyes back to Jennifer's face. "It seemed like such a cruel trick . . . as if life reached out to give me back my happiness and then snatched it away before I could hold it in my hand. You see," he gazed at her steadily. "It was almost like losing her twice. For that one moment when I saw your face, I thought she'd come back to me . . . but when I began to understand that the woman sitting in front of me was someone else . . . I knew that I had lost her forever."

Jennifer stared at the handsome face. That first day, when she had walked into this office he *had* looked at her as if he was seeing a ghost, the ghost of someone he could not forget. She realized now it was the ghost of the woman he loved.

"Justin—" she began gently. He put up a hand to stop her.

"Please," he told her, "I want to tell you everything." He stood up slowly and began to pace around the room.

"We were married when we were very young . . . I was a newspaper journalist and I had just been offered my first job, working on a small paper in Switzerland. We'd only just met, but the thought of going away without her was," he took a deep breath, "impossible. So, I asked her to marry me." He turned and looked into Jennifer's eyes. "We'd only known each other for a few months, but it was enough— that's the way I am." He looked at her closely, "When I fall in love, I know it instantly." Jennifer didn't move. He turned away again.

"We were married immediately . . . and left for Switzerland. Everything was perfect. We were young and in love and both of us were working for the same paper. She was a freelance photographer and we traveled all over the countryside together. She would take the pictures to accompany my stories. We didn't have much money, but it didn't seem to matter . . ."

Jennifer closed her eyes. She had known the kind of love that made shabby apartments beautiful and cheap wine delicious.

Justin's voice continued, "One day, we worked twelve straight hours covering an international film festival. I was very excited about the story and wanted to get it back to the paper for the late edition. We had a tiny, old Alfa Romeo and I was driving like a madman, speeding down winding mountain roads . . . At one point, she asked me to slow down and I got angry with her." His voice stopped suddenly, then he forced himself to go on. "I told her we were news people and news stories were useless unless they were delivered on time. I told her we had to hurry or we would miss the deadline."

He turned to Jennifer, his face a mask of agony.

"The car went around a sharp curve and down a steep incline and there, directly in front of me, was a small car right in the middle of the road. There was a family standing next to it, a couple of kids. I remember my wife screaming and my foot slamming down on the brake, but that's about all . . . I drove the car into the side of the mountain."

Jennifer had stopped breathing. She stared at Justin in horror and could hear it again, the sound of screeching brakes and shattering glass, a sound that would haunt her for as long as she lived.

Justin walked slowly to the huge window and stood looking down at the busy Manhattan street. The afternoon sun cast a golden reflection on his handsome face. His eyes held the torture of remembering.

Jennifer held herself still, trying to think, trying to understand. A picture became clear in her mind. The embassy compound in China, Justin's arms around her and his anguished voice in her ear. She looked down at the picture in her hand. The woman in the car that day, the woman with Jennifer's face.

Monique.

Justin turned to her. He seemed to read her thoughts.

"I wish I could tell you," he said softly, "that she died instantly, but . . . I can't . . ." he turned away. "She lay in my arms for almost an hour, waiting for the rescue squad."

Jennifer looked down at the happy, smiling face in the photograph. Justin's young wife, lying in his arms, broken and bleeding, waiting for help that would come too late.

"Do you know what the last thing was she said to me?" he asked her. She shook her head slowly. "She said 'I forgive you.'" His deep voice broke. Jennifer's eyes filled with tears. She wanted to go to him, to put her arms around him and hold him, but she could not move.

"I *forgive* you!" he said harshly, taking a massive fist and striking the heavy glass of the window. " took her life, I robbed her of everything she had and all she said was, 'I forgive you.'"

Leaning his head forward, he rested it on the cold glass, shutting his eyes. The phone, which had been strangely silent, rang shrilly. Justin turned and looked down into Jennifer's face. He made no move to answer the phone. Eventually, the ringing stopped.

"So you see . . ." his voice was soft and strained "that first day, when you walked into my office, you were not Jennifer Montgomery . . . you were Monique Bradley, my wife, coming back to me."

Jennifer felt the tears slide slowly down her cheeks. His voice continued.

"At first, I couldn't look at you, I couldn't talk to you . . . I knew that I had to keep myself away from you—but I also knew I couldn't let you go, so I hired you."

Jennifer lowered her head and let the tears flow unchecked. Pain and confusion stabbed at her heart. All that time, she thought miserably, all those days and nights when she was thinking about him, falling in love with him, he didn't see her for herself at all, but only as an image of his young wife who died on a mountainside in Switzerland before we'd even met.

Dimly, she was aware that Justin had crossed to the desk and was touching her head, stroking her hair gently.

"But," his voice was deep and warm, "it didn't work . . . I tried to keep away from you, but I knew I couldn't." Jennifer looked up at him. She didn't understand. He reached down and cupped her face in his strong hand. "After I first saw you in the office, I knew I had to get away, to try and sort out my feelings. I went to Europe and tried to throw myself into my work, but it didn't help. I thought about you day and night, remembering your smile and the way it felt to touch you." Justin reached down and pulled Jennifer gently out of the chair. He placed his hands her shoulders. "When I got home, I knew I had to see you again. I was going to show you the picture and explain everything. And then when the elevator doors opened, and I felt you in my arms, when I kissed you, I knew it wasn't Monique I had been

missing all those weeks I had been away . . . bu
you."

Jennifer wanted to move away from him, but hi
arms were suddenly pulling her closer and closer. Sh
struggled to free herself, but she was no match fo
his strength. Why was he doing this? Why was h
telling her more lies? He hadn't been missing her, h
had only been interested in her because she re
minded him of Monique. Jennifer Montgomer
meant nothing to him.

"Justin . . ." she looked up at him, anger displac
ing the sorrow in her eyes, "Let me go . . ."

"No," he told her evenly, "I want you to hear every
thing first. Then you can decide what you want t
do."

She waited impatiently for him to finish his stor
and release her.

"That first time I kissed you," he told her, "I knew
could happen to me again, I knew that the feeling
were still there, even though they had not bee
touched for so long." He looked down into her eyes.
knew if I let myself get close to you, I would fall in lo
with you—and I was afraid, afraid of loving you b
cause to love someone is to risk losing her . . . an
knew I could never bear that kind of pain again."

Jennifer turned her head away from his gaze. Sl
remembered too well the agony she had suffer
when Terry died, the shock and disbelief of realizi
she would never see him again, never kiss him
hold him, the nights of tears and anguish when s
vowed she would never let another man capture l
heart, because she could not bear to have it brok
again.

She did not trust herself to speak. Justin held her gently.

"When I kissed you in the garden, I knew it was you I loved, but I wouldn't let myself believe it, I tried to fight the truth." She was suddenly aware of his nearness, how secure and safe she felt in the circle of his arms. She looked up into his eyes. "And then, I saw Ray kissing you," he said softly. "I saw him put his arms around you and I couldn't deny it any longer . . . I was in love with you."

Jennifer tried to think clearly. That night, the night of the banquet Ray had kissed her, but there was something else. Later, when she fainted . . . she knew she had to ask him, she had to know the truth.

"But, at the embassy—" she began.

"When I saw you fall at the embassy," he said slowly, "it was like a part of my life being lived over again. I held you in my arms and the past and the present were suddenly together, at one place and time.

"I never grieved for Monique. I never let myself mourn for her. I simply buried the past, made myself forget what had happened. I never even told anyone about her. I just tried to believe that she had never existed at all.

"When I held you in my arms, so still and lifeless, something snapped inside me . . . I wouldn't let anyone touch you. You were the most important thing in my life and I was afraid I had lost you before I ever really found you. And I knew something else . . ." He raised his hand slowly and touched Jennifer's tear-stained cheek.

"I knew," he said softly "as my world began to fall apart around me, that one thing was clear." He

157

looked down into her eyes. "I was so afraid of losing you, that I finally let her go . . ."

Jennifer looked up into his eyes, searching their depths for the truth. She wanted so desperately to believe him, but she was afraid to believe he really loved her for herself and not as the image of a haunting memory.

She moved away from him and he did not try to stop her. She remembered something else. That day in China, when Justin had come into her hotel room, he had been out all night and looked exhausted, yet there was a calm serenity about his face that she had never seen before, like a man who is suddenly at peace after many years of turmoil.

She wanted to believe he loved her. She wanted to rush into his arms, but something held her back, one more unanswered question.

"Justin," she turned to where he stood watching her closely, "if I hadn't found the picture, would you ever have shown me what Monique looked like?"

He gazed at her steadily. "I have been asking myself that same question ever since we got back from China," he told her. "I've had that picture buried on my desk for months. It's the only one I kept of her. It took all the strength I had to look at it again. I knew I had to tell you about Monique, about the way she died, but I was afraid if you knew what she looked like, you would never believe I loved you for yourself."

Jennifer looked into his warm blue eyes. There was no mistaking the love they held.

"Jennifer," he said gently, "all I'm asking is that we give it a try, try to forget the past . . . and see if we can make it work together. I want to make you believe

I love you, not some memory, but you . . . Jennifer Montgomery. All I'm asking for is a chance."

She held herself still, searching her heart for the answer. They had both suffered so much, both endured such misery and heartache. Maybe together they could learn the meaning of happiness again.

"A chance . . ." she smiled slowly. "As I remember, that was what I asked you for my first day in this office. Yes, please—let's give our love a chance."

She rushed into his outstretched arms, feeling them pull her toward him in a powerful embrace. He pressed his mouth down on hers, sending waves of delight surging through her body. She reached up, circling his neck with her slender arms, pulling his mouth even closer to hers. As his kisses became more and more demanding, she answered them with all the strength of her love, promising to replace the darkness of his painful memories with all the happiness and joy his heart could hold.

"I love you," he murmured against her cheek. She looked up and saw the love held deep in his eyes and knew, in that one moment, that whatever heartache and pain they had suffered belonged to the past.

She kissed him deeply, surrendering completely.

"Justin, I love you, too," she said softly.

She felt his arms tighten around her, felt his kisses consuming her and knew, as she gave herself to his love, that they were free at last, free from the secrets and shadows of the past, free to enjoy a love that knew no questions or sorrow.